A Picture Painted with Words

A Picture Painted with Words

By J.R.S. Davis

XULON PRESS

Xulon Press
2301 Lucien Way #415
Maitland, FL 32751
407.339.4217
www.xulonpress.com

© 2020 by JRS Davis

All rights reserved solely by the author. The author guarantees all contents are original and do not infringe upon the legal rights of any other person or work. No part of this book may be reproduced in any form without the permission of the author. The views expressed in this book are not necessarily those of the publisher.

Unless otherwise indicated, Scripture quotations taken from the King James Version (KJV) – *public domain*.

Printed in the United States of America.

ISBN-13: 978-1-6312-9348-1

J.R.S. Davis dedicates this project to three heroes: Valerie Colette, Julienne Claire, and Chantrelle Laniece, with hugs, kisses and wonderful memories.

ACKNOWLEDGMENTS

J.R.S. Davis acknowledges first and foremost the Lord Jesus Christ for in him we live, move and have our being. We thank him for giving us the ability to write and the courage to share our thoughts with others. We thank our families for supporting us on our journey. We love you all very much.

Special thanks to Michaela and Sherryanne for being wonderful in more ways than we can express. Also, to Shawn Watson who said, "Chase your dream; you can catch it," and to Isaac J. Naquin and Eula Felder for their thoughtfulness.

James, Rory and Sarah Davis, sincerely thank everyone who will read this book. All of you play an essential role in the success of this project. Thank God for all of you!

Table of Contents

Part I: The Picture Begins 1
    The Soul's Journey
    No Road to Nowhere!
    Bells
    River of Life
    Live Song
    Who?
    Well Known
    Fuel of Thought
    Pros of Procrastination
    We're All Brothers
    All About You
    Breathed into Dirt
    On One Street
    The Innocent One
    Walking in Hope
    While Opportunity is Available
    Why Do You Love Me?
    Enlightenment

Part II: Color Harmony 49
    The Shotgun House
    Love Always Loves
    A View from Above
    Out of My Realm
    Love Would Never Do That!
    God Blessed Life

Gain Through Loss
Smile!
Affection
You
Just Because
Along the Way
Love

Part III: Changing the Brush 82
Be (To Every Man)
He Painted the Wind!
Missing While Being There
I Am That Man
Down by the Stream
In the Season
All About Breath
The Birthday
Reflections
Influence
Guidance
Passing Fields
Meadows and Mountains
The Power of One
Years
My Parting Words

Part IV: Broadening the Brush Strokes 128
Really
Mr. Woodspring
Two Fools
The Road to Friendship
Who Am I?
A Letter to My Friend
My Friend
Sometimes at Night, I Fight

Thoughts
A Better Day!
That's Life
Moving Forward
Where Did Your Thoughts Go?
If
Hello, Happiness
A Different Way
You are a Woman

Part V: Shades, Shadows and Pastels 175

The Standoff
Falsely We Believe
Dark Days
For All
In the Land of Hypocrisy
What's Your Next Move?
The Inside Man
How We See It
Wild Thing
TagTeam Duo
Who's Writing the Lyrics to Your Song?
Just Traveling Through
Out of Touch
Why Do You Settle for Less?

Part VI: Mixing Colors 246

Hope's Expectation
O.W.L.
Just One Taste
Golgotha
Calvary
Man's Question. God's Statement.
Memories
In Light of Eternity

Part VII: Final Touches 283
    Climb On
    Inner Strength
    Special Gift
    Light
    Because of You
    Providence, Fate, and Destiny!
    Two Sides of the Ground
    Temporary

References 317

Introduction

This project is the culmination of three writer's styles and thoughts combined into one idea. Although it stems from three generations' experiences, it's blended into one concept. This project, in its purest form, is a book of poems, poetic thought, and prose. However, it also aims to tell a story—the great story of life with its many substories that come together in it.

Of course, you can read each poem, the prose, and poetic thoughts individually, and I am sure some will do just that. However, our focus is for the reader to read them as a collective body to visualize the complete story.

The titles of the poems, prose, and poetic thoughts were moved to the right of each page except for the titles that lead to the continuation of the narrative. All titles have been underlined to make spotting them more convenient.

We have also chosen not to identify the individual author of any of the thoughts expressed in this project. The project should be viewed solely as "A Picture Painted with Words" by J.R.S. Davis.

We hope that reading this book will be an enjoyable experience for you. It has indeed been a pleasant experience for us while writing each thought and putting those thoughts and expressions in print to be shared with you.

Our prayer is that something in this book will challenge you, encourage you, provoke you, inspire you, and remind you of your story. In all things, we give honor to God. We are very thankful, incredibly grateful, and feel enormously blessed for this opportunity to share with you, *A Picture Painted with Words*.

Part I

THE
PICTURE
BEGINS

The Soul's Journey

A purpose drives my soul
'I must go!'
The words are etched into my heart
'I must go!'
The journey begins
'I'm going!'
My soul shouts with glee
'I'm going!'
The journey of discovery
'I'm searching!'
Looking for the meaning
'I'm searching!'
What is the purpose of life?
'I wonder.'
Is it all that it seems?
'I wonder.'
Life, meaning, questioning, searching;
it's all a part of humanity.

There was a Wise Man who was asked to share his experiences as well as his views on life. So, he contacted some friends and acquaintances and suggested "Invite anyone interested in hearing my story and views to meet me this Saturday at 10:00 a.m. at the Central Town Square building. There I shall meet you and very candidly share my ups and downs, my adventures and my struggles, as well as my concerns."

That Saturday, in transparent detail, the Wise Man in the presence of his peers, acquaintances, friends, and enemies, openly shared his life. As he engaged with them in intimate conversation, intertwining his thoughts with humor and seriousness, he spoke candidly of love, and hate; of joy, and pain; of the adventures he's had and dreams he's fulfilled; and of those dreams he has not yet seen come to fruition.

Life, he says, can be as enjoyable as paradise, however from the choices we make, it can also be disastrous. Therefore, he chose his words wisely while sharing his experiences with us. Come, join him and listen as he paints an intricate picture of life.

"There's no road to nowhere!" began the Wise Man very pointedly. Looking directly into the faces of those gathered with his eyes casually glancing from face to face, he repeated his statement. "There is no road to nowhere! Every path has a destiny. Our lives are about destiny, meaning some things in our lives will happen regardless of what we do or fail to do. However, just as some roads have dead ends, we can take our lives down cul-de-sacs due to our decisions. Every decision brings a reward, consequence or a delay."

The Wise Man smiled and continued sharing his thoughts. "Don't make your life more difficult by trying to work around the things that are inevitable or kicking at troubles when they come. We should also not take the position of making other people's lives harder to make ours better. Blowing out someone's flame shall not make yours shine any brighter. On sunny days and cloudy days, we should smile, and enjoy this life the best way possible. Because it comes with one guarantee: "it will end." In between, the start and finish it's in our hands."

"We all have a ball, baton, hammer, and nails. We get to use that hammer and nails for good or evil, pass our baton or not, and to enjoy our ball, leave it in the corner, share it, or give it to someone else. That's what life is made of: balls; batons; hammers; and nails! He paused, scratched his head, chuckled, and quoted, Lao Tzu (n.d.), "The journey of a thousand miles begins with one step;" and there is certainly no road to nowhere, so …

No Road to Nowhere!

Let us take our journey which goes somewhere
Being bold and courageous enough to declare
We have the freedom to be cautious;
Aware all crossroads, aware that all avenues,
Mindful of all paths or boulevards traveled,
Could be beneficial or dearly cost us.
For there is no such road, "The road to nowhere,"
Every road takes us somewhere,
And our attitude while traveling and when we arrive
Where our path has led us to, we'll see
Is up to you and me
How interesting that man must travel
A way that destiny unravels
Through a plethora of mystery and riddle
That living subjects each man to.
Thus, choosing any road man still learns
From the bumps, and the bends, and the burns,
Of things planned and of things unsuspected.
Plus, life's peculiarities lend some reasons
To not let go of a few memorable seasons
But there are those who view nostalgia as treason
From the present course, that life has selected.
So, as we travel life's road we do find,
A pattern to life by design
A mixture that's coarse and refined;
A way that's kind and unfair.

With trails of deception and truth
And ways of aged wisdom and foolish youth
Plus, many theories established without proof
And days of joy and grief and despair.
Beneath changing skies which are endless
Walking with companions and sometimes friendless
We journey onward compelled or senseless
Always heading somewhere.
By common sense, intellect, or philosophy
Man paring all three won't outwit destiny
Which brings in the earth's sphere its harmony
And takes all humanity somewhere.
For no man has ever found that road,
That mysterious life-long road,
That runs, with dips and bumps and curves,
And leads anyone nowhere.

He had begun painting the picture. And like a cat surveying the room getting the feel of the surroundings, he casually moved forward waving and shaking a few hands. He paused and looked towards the ceiling as if to grab a thought from that element. He shifted his gaze from the ceiling back to us with an intense look of reflection. Then passionately he said, "I remember my childhood. Those years of growing and developing laid the foundation to help me become the person you see standing before you today."

"Life has hit me hard many times" he said reflectively "but thanks to the good foundation I received as a child I never had a quitter's attitude." Then, raising his hand to his ear and leaning forward in the way one does when trying to hear a sound in the distance, he smiled and spoke enthusiastically …

Bells

Shhh! Listen, do you hear that?
Listen! Listen! do you hear that faint sound of bells?
Yes! Bells! Church bells, school bells.
Listen! Do you hear that voice?
Listen! That's my Grandmother speaking!
It's Sunday, and it's nearing time for Sunday school to start.
Can you hear her speak?
She's saying "Git' up boy, putyo' clos' on,
wash yo' face n hans n c'mon n here and eat,
it's nare' time fo' Sunday School to start."
Take a deep breath, do you smell that?
Breathe again, do you smell it? That smell
is breakfast cooking! Fatback, eggs, hot biscuits,
and grits floating in freshly churned butter.
Look! Look! See those jars she just placed on the table?
That's preserves, figs, and watermelon rind.
"C'mon boy hurr' up ya gonna be late if you don't make haste."
I hurried as quickly as I could to wash up and get dressed.
While doing so, I smashed my toe against the bedpost.
I let out a scream that startled grandmother.
Acknowledging my cry, she quipped, "boy,
you bout scared tar nations outta' me.
What you don gone n' don now?"
While rushing through my breakfast
and finishing the biscuit with my favorite preserve,
the watermelon rind, the church bells began ringing.

I stuffed the last bite of biscuit and preserves into my mouth and wiped my mouth with my shirt sleeve,
I then grabbed my Sunday School book and my grandmother's hand. As we rushed out of the door, she scolded me for my improper personal hygiene practices
with "boy, you been taught better n nat, use yo handkerchief."
While rushing off to church, she sang, "Near the Cross."
We approached the church as the bell tolled its last chime.
We entered the doors of the sanctuary
as the ringing sound slowly decreased in intensity.
Listen, can you hear that? That voice?
That's Deacon Young singing the opening song,
"Just a Closer Walk with Thee,"
followed by the morning prayer by Deacon Wilson.
The bell tolled, and we separated and gathered in
individual classes to learn values that would last forever!
The bells of time toll softly in the mind of a man.
The bells toll vividly and loudly in the heart of a man.
The hands of thought are holding on tightly to the rope
of memory that rings the bells of time
in the schoolhouse and chapel in my soul.

Bells deep down in my soul! That's what I remember! And my grandmother's voice lovingly encouraging and correcting me. Some things will stay with you always, he said endearingly."

He paused briefly, shook another hand, moved forward again, still surveying the room and embracing his guests. Stopping near a somewhat insecure-looking teenager standing awkwardly among those listening, he continued sharing his story.

River of Life

I stood by the river of life,
but I was afraid to jump in and learn to swim.
I stood watching the sunrays dancing on the ripples of the water.
I stood there through the days and nights of joy and sorrow.
I watched the moon rise over the treetops
and cast its reflection upon the river.
Still, the fear of drowning in failure ruled my life,
As the moon hid its glow and turned its face
to the mountain and left me standing in the dark,
I turned and stumbled through the brush
and slipped in the washes along the river.
I stumbled through dusk and dawn, season after season.
I skated on the ice when the river was frozen over,
but I always headed for the banks of the river before spring
insuring myself a dry spot along the river.
I dreamed of swimming to the Island of Success,
but the dream always seemed to vanish in the wave of despair
like a stone thrown from the mountaintop.
The winds of time blew steady and sometimes very cold.
And upon the winds of time, I was taken to the cleft
and left standing on a thin and jagged ledge of hope.
The weight of doubt broke the ledge of hope,
and I fell into the water.
My life flashed before my eyes as I was sinking,
drowning beneath the waves.

I started flinging my arms and vigorously kicking my feet,
and suddenly, as though a miracle had saved me,
I realized I was swimming and enjoying it.
Although the water seemed to soothe me,
when I reached the shore, I was exhausted,
yet encouraged to try again.
I now enjoy dunking myself in the river of life,
for it is as essential as the air I breathe.

"You know what's strange," he said reflectively. "My grandmother always spoke empowering words to me yet many times I was overcome with fear. Fear can hold us back from some of the greatest things we will ever experience or accomplish. Life is designed to challenge us to be great, but fear of the unknown, fear of failure, fear of inadequacies, fear of rejection, fear in all of its damaging ways can often grab us and stagnate our progress."

"There are so many different forms of fear that sometimes we don't even realize we are being influenced by it or overcome with it. There is also healthy fear; we call that caution and reverence." He glanced at the ceiling again. "But let's look closer at this tyrant called 'unhealthy fear' which I believe is just as debilitating as cancer and far more dangerous." The Wise Man put one arm up and moved it like a bird's wing, flapped it twice and stopped.

"There was a red-tailed hawk that was afraid of heights and of stretching its wings. Therefore, it didn't fly very high above the ground. All the other hawks encouraged it to fly higher, yet it constantly refused to do so. 'I'm okay with this elevation' was its continuous reply. It's overwhelming fear of the unknown, the uncontrollable, and the vastness of the blue above was keeping it from soaring so that bird just kept flying low in a realm where it felt comfortable, familiar, and somehow safe. What's worse—it convinced a few of its companions to do the same."

"One day, while it was flying barely above the bushes in the forest, a quick-witted fox grabbed that hawk and killed it. Imagine if that bird would have taken the chance on flying higher, it would have spotted the fox and avoided that carnage. Plus, it would have manifested its natural ability, and its fullest potential would have been realized. Sadly, it did not; as its potential had died, consumed by the fox."

"Therefore," repeated the Wise Man, "don't let unhealthy fear trap you. Don't let fear be your dictator; your captor holding you imprisoned in its iron claws. Don't let the anxiety of the unknown or the uncontrollable keep your mind locked up. Do you really have as much control over things as you think you do? Even in the most ideal situations, something could happen beyond your control. So, it's better to attempt and fail than to fear and not try at all because in the attempt you may find you can fly higher than you ever imagined possible."

The Wise Man let out a deep sorrowful sigh, saying, "Fear causes many problems for mankind." He sighed deeply again, still looking at the youth, but it was apparent that he was addressing everyone. "Don't let unhealthy fear bury you, clip your wings, or keep you from expanding to your fullest potential."

The Wise Man shifted his stance, closed his eyes as if he was meditating and said, "one way I deal with anxiety is that I try to look beyond what makes me afraid and focus on something that doesn't. I concentrate on the things that bring joy and peace. I think about lovely things, things that are true and of a good report, as Paul said we should do in his letter to the Philippians (KJV). I keep those thoughts as a compass." He opened his eyes glanced at the youth again and extended his hand to him and stated, "we have to learn to live without fear" then with warmth in his eyes he proceeded

Live Song

I awake each morning with thanksgiving.
I read a Bible verse and think about death or the other side.
Sometimes I wonder if, when I'm there, will I write live songs?
I want to live my life in a manner that is loving and giving, and
peaceful and tranquil while I'm here.
But when I'm gone, I want to write a live song!
As I reach an intersection in life and interact with others
year by year, in my interactions, may I write a live song
for someone to carry when I'm no longer here…
When I depart, be it in death or merely leaving
from among you to travel to another intersection
to interact with another that I've never met,
will you smile and say farewell, there goes a friend?
If so, then I have written a live song!

He smiled at the insecure teenager again and said, "live songs are hard to write when unhealthy fear is present. Unhealthy fear is always trying to destroy our peace and hinder our progression. Therefore, I remind myself of fear's many traps and how those traps produce negativity, and how negativity can ignite more fear. To fight fear, I embrace change, and embrace people with love. I do my best to stay moving in the right direction, trying to be optimistic in all of my interactions. Unfortunately, as I stated earlier, there have been moments when fear, insecurity, doubt, and anxiety have grabbed me and gripped me tightly. But the blessing is in those moments; I confess to God that I am afraid, and I ask Him to help me not be frightened. The power of His word and the encouragement of His promise takes the fear away and gives me wings again."

The Wise Man placed his hand on the shoulder of a man standing next to the youth and said, "If I can be an inspiration in someone's life, if I can help them overcome their fears and insecurities, or help them achieve their goals, it gives my day a greater sense of purpose, a grander focus on living. Because extending love and a helping hand to others is another way, I overcome fear and continue writing a live song."

He removed his hand from the man's shoulder. "Can anyone here admit that fear tries to grab you from time to time? Can anyone admit that fear tries to entangle you in its web? I'm convinced fear has crippled more people than diseases ever will." The Wise Man looked reflectively and said "I would grow every day in my battle with uncertainty. However, I must confess there was a time in my life when I was so uncertain about so many things that I asked myself these questions

Who?

Who am I?
Where is God?
Who is God?
Where am I?
Am I lost?
Why am I lost?
Am I really lost?
Or is there no place or anyone else?
God,
Can you hear me?
God,
Will I join you there?
I smell roses,
magnolias and honeysuckle.
Is that you, God?
I see blue skies,
Tall, green trees adorned with beautiful, fluttering leaves,
and a blue-green meadow.
Is that you, God?
I hear rushing waters, the surf beating against the rocks,
is that you, God?
I feel the sea breeze rushing past me,
carrying time rushing with it.
Is that you, God?
Look! Look, there's an antelope
dashing through the forest,

or,
was that you, God?
Oh,
what was that?!
Was that thunder, and that bright flash
that just streaked the sky
like Jupiter's comet?
Was that you, too, God?
I see dark clouds and with them come rain.
I see the birds that serenade me with beautiful songs, fleeing
for shelter.
There are all types of animals doing the same,
and I smiled
because tomorrow, be it one day or one week,
the sun will shine again.
Is that you, God?
Or is that *because* of you?
Are you one God, or are you all the things
that I see, feel, hear, smell, and touch?
Where are you, God?
Who is God?
Where am I?
Who am I?
Why?

Moving away from the man and the insecure-looking teenager who was shifting a bit nervously with his hands shoved in his pockets, he continued. "These were very pertinent questions that were eating at me. Those same questions may be nagging some of you. Questions like, "Who is God? Where is God? Are you one God? Or are you all the things I see, feel, hear, smell or touch? I wanted answers immediately.

Maybe you do as well!" The Wise Man smiled thoughtfully and continued. "All my questions weren't answered immediately but what I discovered in my search was amazing—a truth discovered by faith. The reality that God knows me, understands me, and all of my uncertainties. And that He lovingly reaches out to me daily to make Himself better known. This is what my grandmother was trying to convey to me for many years, that God completely understands us even when we don't grasp the reality of Him.

That's why I can look up now in gratitude and say...

Well Known

God,
I'm glad you know me;
And Lord,
You really know me
 much better than I know me;
 plus, your viewpoint is true.
And even though you know me,
 you still take time to show me
 that although you truly know me,
 you love me through and through.
And Father,
I know you know me,
 and continuously you show me
You intend to grow me,
 that I'll be more like you.

"So, I repeat with great joy" said the Wise Man smiling, "God knows everything about me down to the smallest detail. And He still stretches His hands to me—in my fears, insecurities, and doubts. He doesn't ridicule me for my questions or my shortcomings but does everything to make me a better person. He makes everything work for my good.

And the natural world He placed around me is so I can behold a portion of His greatness in a visible way. His majesty is displayed everywhere."

"Therefore, I believe in everything we do, we should be more like God's thought of us, more like God's clear view of us, and more like his actions towards us."

"We should let his prevailing wisdom and loving affection motivate and guide us each day. That calms every fear and helps us to view others and ourselves in the proper light. This brings me back to the bells of my foundation. God's love is a bell. And trusting the Lord gets rid of fear, whatever the fear is."

"What's your biggest fear?" The nervous youth asked the Wise Man abruptly. The Wise Man was caught off guard by his sudden question. "My biggest fear?" the Wise Man said, repeating the question unwittingly. "Hmm, my biggest fear? Well, I have always had two major concerns: the fear of being shaped into this world's mentality is one and the other is the fear of falling away from God's truth. Those two thoughts have always challenged me. But as I said, trusting the Lord gets rid of unhealthy-fear, and keeps us on the right track." The Wise Man looked away from the youth and inhaled deeply. He positioned himself on a nearby stool and continued with sad passion and endearing conviction in his voice.

Fuel of Thought

I was sitting quietly in my little office.
My energy was smoldering when I realized that I was burning the fuel of thought.
In my thoughts were war, peace, love, joy, hate, sadness, pain, misery, comfort, shelter, glamour, beauty, and ugliness.
As well as hunger, honor, deceit, gluttony, religion, spirituality, there was also ignorance, education, stupidity, and brilliance.

These things burn in the minds of millions of people by the seconds. I thought of the teachings of God.
God teaches with absolute honesty, precision, and consistency.
Science and our educational system refer to Him as Mother Nature.
Nature, as it is defined is "the natural world as it exists without human beings or civilization."
After reading that definition, more fuel began burning.
Is man unnatural?
Did not human beings arrive from the same source?
I can see that the teachings of man are not always without bias or an ulterior motive.
The information conspiracy repeatedly teaches us their ways.
And if we speak and write the bias views of psychiatrists,
bishops, pastors, and teachers with Ph.D.s, MBAs, and BAs long enough, it will sound like, feel like,
and perform like the truth.

We need to put our corporal senses aside
and burn the weightier fuel of thought.
Set ablaze the propaganda and consider
Why is so much fuel of thought burned on creating war
and war machinery?
Why is so much fuel of thought used on thinking up lies,
and, ways to cheat, trick, and deceive each other?
Why is so much fuel of thought used to camouflage reality
and keep the public in a tunnel?
These tactics have been temporal at best.
From the dark ages through today, one would think
that modern man with all the technical knowledge
would have learned that little ditty.
Many teach love and practice hate;
teach peace and practice war;
teach fairness and practice injustice.
Maybe they should teach war and practice peace?
Teach injustice and practice fairness;
teach hate, and practice love?
The burning of my fuel of thought suggests
that this is worthy of a try!

A petite redhead with granny framed glasses and matching rose-colored lip gloss asked the Wise Man a question, "Do you believe that mankind can make the adjustments necessary to restructure their lives for the better?"

"Of course, I do," he replied. "We have the power within us to do better things, and we can be better people if our lives are surrendered to Christ's help and rule. However, this sad reality confronts us daily; people are habitual."

Pros of Procrastination

People in general
have a tendency to say,
"I'll do that-one tomorrow."
We move that one to a later date,
As if we had time to borrow.
Never considering that something else
could suddenly get in the way,
And once again that critical thing
will, unfortunately, face another delay.
Procrastination,
beautiful procrastination,
you feel so good
to our slothfulness.
Procrastination,
sly procrastination,
keeping us off balance
with busyness.
Was it idleness or
was it busyness?
That would not allow progression
towards so many things we have said we'd do
that never came to completion.
We keep on shoving things
towards tomorrow
that could have been accomplished yesterday.
But sadly, there it comes again.

Clever procrastination
getting right in the way.
"I'm gonna do it," I'm gonna do it,"
Seems to be most folk's battle cry!
And if people would delay hatred, bigotry, selfishness,
like they postpone everything else,
fewer innocent people would die.
So, procrastination could have a positive side,
if it preserves human existence.
But any other form of procrastination
should be met with the most
determined resistance.

"Therefore, to answer your question more specifically, yes, I believe humanity can change for the better. However, I also think we must begin now without delay, without excuses, and with this simple concept in mind that we all stem from one human family. And if we view it from that perspective, we shall act differently toward each other." The Wise Man continued his thoughts. "Have you ever noticed?

We're All Brothers

Some Asians resemble Mexicans
And some Mexicans look like Africans
While Africans resemble Americans
in one way or another.
Occasionally, Chinese look like Russians
and Russians can favor Arabians.
Plus, Arabians are like American Indians
And their Asian-Indian brothers.
The Japanese could be Alaskans,
Alaskans could be Cambodians, and
Cambodians could be Ethiopians.
If you get an opinion from me,
some quiet similarities
can be found in every country,
can be found in every race.
throughout every nationality,
some features of the African
can be seen in the Asian,
can be seen in the European, and
can be seen in the Australian.
The facial structure found in England
that may be seen in Thailand,
that may be seen in Holland,
could be present on a Jamaican.
For some Caucasians have thick lips,
and some Negroes have delicate noses,

and some Asians are very tall.
But this is not what bias poses.
Some Russian's are petite,
every Swede is not blonde,
all Sudanese are not dark,
and all Cambodian's physiques are not small.
The consensus may certainly be
there are certain physical traits
found predominately in each race.
Yet, it can be seen from nation to nation
a quiet similitude presented by
some similarity in each face.
While each race has some features
that are present to demonstrate
the distinctive differences from the others;
every race has some features
that are present to prove
the grand and glorious beauty
that we are all uniquely brothers.

"You see," said the Wise Man, "we are all brothers connected by blood. All in one big human family. And if we look closer, beyond our bias and stereotyping of one another, we can see it, that sameness from person to person regardless of the skin color.

We should know that the appearance and charm of a person do not indicate a person's character. Some of the worst people in society have looked innocent and have had great personalities.

While others may have looked ugly and awkward but were some of the noblest people to ever meet. I am not trying to insult anyone's intelligence by stating the obvious, but this certainly proves that the speed of a horse cannot be determined by looking at its color.

"Therefore, we must stop allowing preconceived ideas to shape our views of people. Not all blacks are bad, and not all whites are good. There are innocent and guilty folk, as well as caring and despicable people in every race. There are moral and immoral people of every nationality and cruel and kind people in every ethnic group, without exception." The Wise Man rubbed his hands together and continued. "Character building is a daily process because we are continuously growing and evolving into what we choose to be or finding out what God says we should be and following that course. The potential for greatness is in every human; all possess the innate ability to become anything life has to offer." The Wise Man sneezed twice, said "excuse me," and continued. "It's up to everyone to be the best they can. It's not my responsibility to make you better, nor is it your responsibility to make me better."

"We can assist one another in the process of becoming better and challenge each other to be better. However, that's all, we cannot make anyone better by force. We do not possess that power; such power belongs only to God. He holds that kind of strength, and he does not force his ways or will on anyone either, so, how can we?" The Wise Man smiled, sneezed again and then said, "It's their choice! We may have different exteriors, but our interiors can be the same, displayed by the choices we make, and the lives we live."

"Furthermore," he smiled again, then added, "Please, do not pretend to be someone that you are not. I have learned," the Wise Man said, rubbing his face in a slow, deliberate way. "Nobody likes a phony, a hypocrite, or those that put-on airs, attempting to make themselves seem more significant than they are or at least more prominent than the next person. Therefore, my suggestion has always been to one and all ...

All About You

Be you!
Nobody can be you
better than you can.
Besides, anyone trying to be
someone else
reduces one's self to a
second-hand duplication
of another person.
And everyone,
is one
outstanding,
one-of-a kind,
unique,
original,
Individual.
Being ...
created in the image
of God
and given a chance to be
a beautiful reflection of that image.

"God's reflection is the best image to project. Believe me, God is not looking for robots or cheap imitations, and genuine people don't like it either. I have discovered in my journey" said the Wise Man smiling, "The Lord sees beyond the illusion we present and meets us in our reality. Which means, he meets us, not our idea of us! So, we must accept ourselves, our limitations, our inadequacies, our shortcomings, and be grateful for our qualities, abilities, and gifts. The combination of these positive and negative factors speaks of who we are; and if we don't embrace both sides realistically, we become imbalanced in our view of ourselves and others. Consider this, when we pretend to be someone other than our true selves, we don't give the people we encounter the opportunity to meet us; they meet our façade. And a front is always strenuous to hold up. So, if you want to be your best, allow the Lord to shape your ways, then you can be the best you possible."

The Wise Man rubbed his chin in the same deliberate motion that he had rubbed his face. Then, moving his hand from his chin to his head, he stroked it, as if that motion would bring forth some locked away memory he wanted to share. He paused for a second; his body was almost motionless, except for the slight movement of his hands on his head. His eyes wandered from face to face of the onlookers that watched him; then, as if some invisible hand had pushed him forward and propelled him to continue, he expressed his belief.

Breathed into Dirt

From the dust of the earth,
the man was taken.
From that same dust, the man was formed
by the hand of God into what we now see
in all its beautiful diversity.
People with fascinating personalities,
people with many different languages,
people of all types of cultures,
and so many interesting nationalities.
Not even two people share the same identity;
not even two people
with the same fingerprints.
The teeth of every human are slightly different
and no two people leave the same footprints.
Everyone has a unique voice,
everyone has a distinctive face,
my ears and your ears are not the same
though they're sitting in the same common place.
On our heads dimensionally, set back from our nose,
and not just attached there to take up space.
But with delicate precision, they were positioned
gracefully at the side of the face.
It's incredible that from one single act,
life was given to such defined handiwork
which transpired in that solitary moment
when God breathed His uniqueness into the dirt.

The Wise Man paused and took another deep breath which sounded more like a perplexed groan, then, with a thoughtful expression, continued the narrative. "Although we were all made by the same Creator, individuality makes every person unique. God planned it that way. He also planned for each person to discover their true identity, and uniqueness in Him. Unfortunately, that's not always the case because we live on this big blue planet of imperfect people that struggle with identity and accepting themselves at times and what God has for them, in Him."

"I have had the blessing of meeting a variety of people," the Wise Man said as he gently rubbed his forehead. "I've met the pretenders and, on the other hand, those who are so straight-forward their transparency is almost shocking. I have encountered folk who smile in a storm, and people who complain on bright sunny days with a biscuit in their hand, fussing about the food. I've met all types of people on one street. Yes, I have! All sorts of people," he repeated with an under the breath groan, as if to validate his comments. Then, with a weary smile he continued, "you may have discovered as I have …

On One Street

There's a joyful old person with no legs,
There's an angry young person with two.
There's a woman that's praying
for one child,
and another who has abandoned a few.
There's one child
who is engulfed with love.
There's a youth that's been taught only hate.
There's a man
who avoids any argument,
and there's another who seeks out debate.
There's a female who feels she's so ugly,
and there's another who thinks she's divine.
There's a slothful person in every city,
and there's at least one
that doesn't waste time.
There's a gentleman who has very little;
He's been laughing about it for years.
There's a guy in a mansion
that has great possessions
and daily cries bitter tears.
There's a poor child
that doesn't hold sadness,
and there's a rich kid
That doesn't have joy.
There are some children with too many playthings,

and some children don't have a toy.
So, I thought about all the people
from the least fortunate to the very elite,
and found to be sound
in every country around,
both could be found on the same street.

"Healthy and sick, happy and sad, all in the same vicinity with their personalities, individuality, attitudes, and concerns."

"I am grateful to have encountered so many different types of people in my life; it gave me a better view of humanity, and it helped me to not be judgmental and caused me to be grateful. It gave me more compassion for the less fortunate and showed me the beauty of contentment. There are many discontented people in this world who have no compassion or empathy."

The Wise Man paused reflectively and continued, "Contentment, empathy and compassion are qualities I'd like to see in everyone, but that's not how it is." He sighed deeply and said, "But, I won't give up the hope for these qualities to be developed in people everywhere."

Then, with kindness in his eyes, he let his gaze land on a young mother holding her baby lovingly in her arms. Her other child pulled at her dress, craving more attention. Right next to her was the insecure looking young man with the sad eyes and a middle-aged woman wearing a pastel dress that revealed too much cleavage. Ironically, the young woman was wedged between insecurity and vanity while the child yanked on her dress. She pulled both her children closer, and though she seemed a bit weary, there was an undeniable look of deep love and care that the Wise Man noticed. He spoke very intently to the crowd as he shared ...

The Innocent One

There's a heartbeat in the sperm-egg connection,
humans can't initially hear,
for it cannot be detected with the natural human ear.
Nor can it in its first stage of life
be heard with the most advanced medical device.
And although you can't hear it, it's very much alive
and trying with all its energy to survive.
Help it. Don't hinder it.
And please don't consider it
unworthy of living and give
it every possible chance to succeed
for it is a life.
A life that no one ever asks
if it wants to be sacrificed.
You may feel dismayed because your pregnancy came
through lust's attraction.
And maybe you were forced by some male
seeking his immoral satisfaction.
And maybe you feel like it will stop your career
and perhaps it's causing you a lot of anxiety, stress or fear.
But whether it happened in the back seat of a car,
or the backroom of grandma's house,
or in the restroom of some dimly lit bar,
it doesn't matter if the sperm met the egg
in the marital bed, or you committed adultery and got caught.
Don't ever forget, please don't ever forget that

it's not the baby's fault!
For there's a heartbeat in the sperm-egg connection
that you may have missed.
And despite any pain you feel or in light of whatever
is pushing you to abandon this child ...
life is there. It is a person and very much alive.
Give it a chance you got, just a chance to survive.
Give it the same chance you got, the simple opportunity
to survive!

"Life is so precious," he said, "and children are one of the most precious gifts in life. It blesses my heart to see happy children in a loving, safe environment. We have so many children that need a home and too many children being aborted or abandoned."

"Let's pray that all children will someday have safe environments to live in and that women won't consider abortion an option. For without children, there is no future, and humanity will inevitably fade away."

He smiled once more in the direction of the young woman and then, with a small waving gesture of his hand, he beckoned an acquaintance to come forward. Everything about her said determined as she moved towards the platform. He helped her up as she climbed the two steps. He hugged her briefly and shook her hand.

"Thank you so much for your support," she said. He smiled warmly and replied, "you're welcome, Luana! You're very welcome!" Recalling the event that they once attended together to support local groups to generate funds, he reflectively shared that day's phenomenon.

Walking in Hope

Over 9000
soul-powered pedestrians
gathered in Lafayette
with a singleness of heart
and a unified mind.
All
walking, running, hoping,
that there would soon be an end
to the covert monster
which has disfigured and disheartened
many women for many years.
Some walked with the vitality
of imminent hope just around
the next corner or next street.
Others trotted along determined
as though the day held
the ultimate cure for life.
The excitement of high expectation was
buzzing in the air and popping
like a live electrical wire.
There was a symphony of voices gathered in different groups,
all conversing, discussing and chatting
about the same subject in different ways.
There were no Supermen or women of steel there,
but nothing was more heroic,
nothing more potent as their faces

full of faith and belief
as they each made monumental strides and
historical steps towards the finish line.
Confident that they were crushing the enemy
under their feet
and lifting every possible victim up in victory
right in the face of that heartless monster—
breast cancer.

"Yes, we walked that day," he said, smiling, recalling the moment.

"We all celebrated each other with the oneness that invigorates the very heart and soul of a man. My heart was glad for the cheerful victims that had risen above the ashes of defeat and smiled in the face of their fire, while encouraging others to do the same. Yes, we walked, and we were alive, and I left there that day with a heart full of joy and gratitude because that experience enlarged my world and broadened my horizon."

"Luana is a real soldier. She's a trooper with angelic qualities. A soldier above the bar, that's what she is! Her courage in the face of her challenges is phenomenal. Knowing her has been a great motivator, a great blessing—like a real gift from heaven! And although her journey has been arduous, she has embraced it with so much enthusiasm and positivity that I see her as a role model. Embrace those around you that have impacted your lives, give them their soup while they can eat it." He hugged her again, long and endearingly. As she walked down the steps, his eyes were glossy as he smiled warmly at her. He walked back to his stool, took a sip of water, wiped his eyes, and continued with another provoking thought of challenging sentiment.

While Opportunity is Available

Love people now!
Tomorrow is not promised!
It's far beyond our reach,
far beyond our view.
And as we journey through this temporal
headed towards moments
that we may never see,
be it sunrise or sunset
the clock moves in a progression,
offering only the opportunity
to live in that moment's reality.
So, seize every moment with your power,
like it's the only second,
you'll ever experience in time.
And let the intent of you sharing anything,
in every brief but extensive instance,
be as a valentine you freely offer,
considering it could make an essential difference
in their life and yours.

"Generously give to others," said the Wise Man seriously. "Because somebody needs what you have to offer. Always remember," he said kindly, "love and gentleness, patience and kindness are all godly virtues, which yield significant returns." He sighed deep and thoughtful, then uttered his thoughts like a prayer.

Why Do You Love Me?

Lord,
Why do you love me so much?
I'm fallible,
and yet you stay close to me
and love on me as though
I was perfect.
I'm undeserving of your love.
Occasionally, my thoughts drift into areas
that are impure.
My lips say very foolish things.
Sometimes my actions
are not governed by kindness,
gentleness, patience, or the virtues
that I know you love.
Things that I don't need
are often the very things I desire!
That which you want for me
I also crave,
but then lack the motivation,
the courage, the tenacity to pursue it or
the strength to keep pushing until I get
what you have said is already mine to have.
Sometimes it appears
the weight of life is just too heavy.
And yet, I feel your patience,
gentleness, kindness,

and love softly swaying me
and gently saying to me,
"Be encouraged, I am not finished with you yet.
You are clay in my care being shaped by my hands,
and I shall never remove my hands from you,
because you are mine."
Lord, why do you love me so much?

He finished expressing his deep sentiment to God, then stretched his neck and arms, rolled his shoulders, and wiped his eyes once more. "Ahhh, that felt good! God knows and loves me, and I'm grateful for that. And God knows and loves the cancer patient and the disabled person. The junkie and the one that has aborted a child. He doesn't always agree with our actions, and he severely hates our sin, but he dearly loves us all. That's how he is; loving, forgiving, and generous. And though we may not have such pressing issues as someone else, God doesn't love them less or more than he loves us. God doesn't love according to conditions or circumstances that we have or face. He loves us because he is love. How he extends his love to mankind is often mistaken or misunderstood, but he always acts in love."

The Wise Man's head turned to the direction of the door as a young family walked in. Then, smiling broadly, he said, "God sincerely loves you and me equally."

"How can you say God loves us equally?" asked the short, stout man with the New York Yankees baseball cap and matching short-sleeved shirt. "Look at this world and all the mishaps in it and the unfairness; it doesn't look like God loves equally to me! Sometimes, it doesn't look like God loves us at all!

Does anyone else feel like I do?" There were some nods of agreement, others wore looks of disagreement and concern, and scattered here and there were those that appeared neutral, and then someone hollered, "God doesn't exist!" Mixed emotions filled the air. A kaleidoscope of feelings reflecting from the different opinions projected on each face.

The Wise Man moved forward, positioned his body in the way men do when they want to make a serious point. Looking at the man with the Yankees cap, then slowly looking around the room, he said very frankly, "I believe there is one true God!

I believe he loves all humanity. I believe he gives all people a choice to believe Him or not to believe Him. However, He tells us trusting Him is the best way to live, but he will not force himself on us. And the tragedies we see around us have nothing to do with God not loving us. So, this will be our position. I won't force my beliefs on you, and you do the same towards me. But here's my challenge to you, my friend, and to all that are here with any doubt about God's love or His existence. Prove that there is no God and that he doesn't love you and I'll share in your sentiments 100%. But I don't want theory, I want proof!"

"How can I prove that?" the man with the Yankee's cap asked.

"How? That will be on you" said the Wise Man. "And before you mention it, I don't have to prove he exists. I'm only required to believe it." The Wise Man glanced from face to face of all the guests and took a stance in the middle of the podium and spoke as if he were expressing his statements to the eternal God of love.

Enlightenment

Incomprehensible! That's you, Lord, when we
Try grasping your mind, your ways, your love,
with our human intellect and prowess.
However, you—all wise, gentle; loving—
give us an inlet, a gateway, a bridge,
a door straight to your throne
and all your precious promises.
When we act in faith,
you reach out to us,
settle our minds with your wisdom, and
comfort our hearts with your love;
Wipe us off in your mercy and
strengthen us by your power.
Then, placing peace in our soul,
joy in our core,
humility in our spirit,
and hunger in our hearts for all you have to offer,
you teach us how to walk.
Not by sight, mental capacity, or emotion,
but through the strength of believing you.
Your unlimited mercy and grace draw us even closer
and it helps us to trust you completely.
Not with our great intelligence
or any worldly intellect,
because reaching for you with that limited capacity
makes you unreachable and incomprehensible

and blocks us from seeing your love.

The vibrations of emotions in the room were moving from person to person. The diverse views were causing that ripple effect, and the thoughts expressed were generating powerful energy. The Wise Man cleared his throat and said, "Listen! Listen! My friends and acquaintances, I'm not here to challenge your beliefs; I'm here to share mine! You make your own choices, and those choices will come with rewards or consequences. My friend Luana has cancer, as you just heard, and she says God loves her even in her painful condition. That helps me see more clearly his great love for me and reinforces what I believe. It encourages me when I feel down that although I have weary days and days of great trouble, a loving God is watching over me with great concern and empathy in my pain. A God that has grand plans for me, better than the ideas that I have for myself. And as I go through hardships, I know he is loving me and gently holding me in my trials. He goes with me all the way through the struggles. He doesn't drop me or dash out when things get hot and uncomfortable."

The Wise Man continued, "in all of the tragedies that have happened in this world, God has not turned away but has loved all humanity right in the middle of their misery. Yet, he is most times blamed for the problem and rarely seen as the one that keeps the tragedy or trouble from being worse than it is."

"There can always be worse," stated the Wise Man emphatically.

"Thank you again, Luana, for being such an encouragement in my life and the lives of others."

"I'm going to pause for a few moments," he said. "But I shall continue shortly." Discussions were still reverberating in the room. Waves here and there, reverberating waves here and there. Walking towards a muscular man leaning casually against the door post that led to the adjoining room, he asked him, "is the restroom occupied?" The man responded, "Yes, this one is. But there's another one down the hall, that way," and pointed in the direction he should follow.

Part II

COLOR HARMONY

He returned to the area and sat partially on the stool, with one foot resting on the bar at the bottom of it and the other foot lightly on the floor. He had an expression on his face that reflected sincerity, the look of a man that had considered something earnestly and wasn't sure how to express it. His fiery eyes were dancing with intensity. He curled his lips inward and looked at the man who had given him directions to the men's room, and then glanced in the direction of the man wearing the Yankee's cap.

Moistening his lips with a quick flick of his tongue, he said, "while away, I thought about our discussion and of my childhood. Those days of growing up and how that also showed me God's love." He paused, then continued, "I may not be able to relate to everyone's view of life or have enough time to debate all the reasons which have led to your conclusions. However, I believe as I share these next thoughts with you, you will have a better understanding of my position and how it was developed." He glanced around the room and continued.

The Shotgun House

The shotgun house to some is a symbol of disdain
and shame; to others pride, joy, and yes, sometimes pain.
I grew up in a shotgun house. Our bathtub was used as a washtub, a canning cooker, and water heater. The stove for cooking was a wood burner, a giant black thing that would turn red when overheated but the meals that were prepared with it were somewhere close to heaven.
Plumbing did not exist; the water was brought in by bucket from a spring about a hundred yards down in the woods.
Later, we dug a well, and it was somewhat closer,
but the winter months were quite challenging.
The ground would freeze over and that created slick, slippery paths to travel. At night, we used slop jars that had to be emptied each morning because the toilet was an exterior system; that is another story within itself.
The roof was made of corrugated steel which allowed excessive leaking whenever it rained.
With the roof leaking horribly, we had to sleep in shifts to cart out the many pots and buckets strategically arranged throughout and around the house, positioned to catch the rhythmic drips and drops of rain that formed a water symphony. The flooring unfortunately wasn't any better than that of the roof. It was made of wood, and the spaces between the planks seemed as wide as plow rows. They acted as wind tunnels, allowing the wind to howl and whistle to the rhythm of the raindrops that splashed throughout the night.

I can't forget that old fireplace! It would warm your front while that playful and naughty wind would blow up the back of the girls' dresses and run up the pant legs of the boys while massaging and chilling our backsides.

Attempting to keep warm front and back, you had to turn so often it would made you dizzy, and all too frequently turning our backsides to the fire resulted in dire consequences.

Sometimes our clothing became too hot or worse caught fire, and after the dance and a few overturned pots and buckets, and a whipping for our carelessness, which resembled an initiation into a secret society, we carried on with more caution. Occasionally, there would be a delightful treat waiting to soothe the effect of the whipping.

The poignant fragrance of sweet potatoes roasting in the ashes had a way of diverting our thoughts to the moment when we would consume one of those soothing tubers.

But, retrieving them from the ashes was like a rescue attempt while under an attack from heavy artillery fire. That old fireplace could fire off cinders with such fury and accuracy that learning to dance was not an option!

The walls of that old shotgun house were covered with catalog pages from Sears Roebuck and Montgomery Wards. The paste was made of flour and water. Most of our clothes were made from cloth that was ordered from one of those stores.

"Year after year I dreamed of getting away from that shotgun house and never seeing it again, even though, like the weapon it was named after it fired off projectiles that became doctors, lawyers, judges, preachers, teachers and a whole host of other professions. In that shotgun house, we ate together three meals a day, and each of those meals was received with thanksgiving."

"We entertained ourselves and each other with songs and praise. We would gather around the radio and listen to quartet singers, and the Joe Lewis fights. Eventually, we all left that old shotgun house and purchased homes of our own."

"Large homes, two stories high, four bathrooms, six bedrooms, with formal dining areas, huge master bedrooms, and a T.V. in each room. As we ate in shifts, we hardly noticed each other in those vast abodes, I came to realize that I lived in a mansion back when I called that old shotgun house my home because in that little Old Shotgun House, there was love."

As he remembered those former days, his face was a kaleidoscope of emotions. He coughed to regain stability in his voice, then spoke these encouraging words.

Love Always Loves

Follow love.
It is good and glorious not murky or muddy.
And although it seems muddled,
and you feel befuddled,
it is never confused.
It extends graciously,
expands hearts miraculously,
and it always lights a fuse.
It is straight in its direction,
gives true affection and
directs souls to choose.
Paths divine in intent
as it lends encouragement
to all that find it with or without controversy.
Love is the embodiment of kindness
compassion and concern;
the merit that all should learn.
And generously extend
love smooth's out rough edges and
covers many errors while
it molds and shapes and mends
the lives of all who encounter it
so that they in every way benefit
from a genuinely true love.
It's not like lust or infatuation those infamous impostors
impersonating love's sincerity

like crows pretending to be doves.
True love cannot be faked,
and it will not be forged,
and it cannot be conjured.
But it enters a heart
and it expands within a soul,
then it's sincerely pondered.
And all who journey its path
and all who travel its way
will gather this point of view/
Love will never deny itself,
Love will never abandon itself.
And if you cease pursuing it
it will still be beckoning you.

"Love will still be beckoning you" he repeated affectionately.

His eyes were filled with kindness and he appeared to be wrestling with his thoughts and fighting to keep himself balanced. The memories of his youth, the recollections of the shotgun house and what it meant to him had stirred up deep sentiments. He was shifting on the stool like a child trying to find a comfortable spot on his grandpa's knee, and then, a faint, barely audible chuckle somehow escaped his mouth.

He spoke a bit louder—a Shotgun House Full of Love—that's what I remember! The love of God was there! The love of family was there! Love and respect were there! He blinked his eyes reflectively and said love is always worth following, and we should pursue it and share it faithfully." His words had landed on everyone and were fastened to them like tacks to hold a picture on a wall. Everyone was curious about what he would share next. His words caught the crowd by surprise.

A View from Above

From up there
where the eagle's nest,
you're no closer to God
then we who are living
down here
where the turtle's nest.
Your thoughts are lofty;
expensive cars, houses—
you want it all nothing less.
Swimming pools, golf courses,
designer clothing only the best.
Your view is from above,
but where is love?
What has happened to love?

As he glanced around the room, it was quite clear to him by their expressions what was running through their minds. Several faces had that, "Why did he say that? Who's he talking to?" look on them. Questions had become their oxygen, and they were breathing it in deeply.

Maybe his words had stunned them because of the dialogue about God's love and the controversy it had caused; or perhaps it was because now it seemed that he had challenged someone directly concerning their love. It was hard to say what had really happened. The only clear thing was the confusion on some of their faces, and those who were attempting not to look too obvious as they glanced around the room trying to discover who the Wise Man was talking about, or perhaps talking to in code.

Who? What? And why? was hanging in the air, and curiosity was buzzing in the room like a bunch of honeybees, however, the Wise Man didn't entertain their prying. Instead, he took a deep breath to clear his mind then took a slightly different approach and shared these reflections.

Out of My Realm

I once knew a king who went to the mountaintop. I was so impressed I decided to follow him, but when I reached halfway, I looked down and realized things were terribly out of focus. So much so that I decided to come down and circle the mountain from a viewpoint that I could work in, not one out of my realm. Therefore, if you must go to the mountain, do not climb higher than you can keep in focus on reality.

No one moved for a few seemingly eternal moments as they reflected on the tactfully used parable. To some degree it worked in alleviating unnecessary questions, however, one fella eventually spoke up.

"You made us curious," he said quite pushy. "Yeah," agreed a few others. The Wise Man replied thoughtfully, "Some things wouldn't be useful to know, and some things would cause more problems than it is worth to know them. Besides, how will you benefit from this knowledge, and how do you plan to use it?

And furthermore, we just segued from our discussion of God's love into the realm of human love, so how would divulging information that shouldn't be shared with everyone show any compassion to a person or persons that deserve to have their business anonymous?"

"I do apologize," continued the Wise Man "for whetting your appetites, but I shall not become unkind and stoop beneath my principles to satisfy your curiosity. That would not show kindness; on the contrary, that would be quite rude! And I am 100% certain...

Love Would Never Do That!

Love would never do that,
treat anyone like an unwanted stepchild
it wants to embarrass.
This is a fact —
exposing someone's weaknesses, flaws, failures,
for leverage are never acts of love
but are the ways of those whose hearts are calloused.
Love won't seek its own benefit,
never does it grab for self-gratification.
It's not out for a profit
like lust which is motivated by
greed and other sensations.
Love wants what's best for all
and endeavors to fulfill their needs.
Love will always stand tall;
it won't lie dormant
or become stagnant and still,
and even if you don't detect it
due to your lack of discernment
or blindness,
love will always be there.
It reveals itself without comment
in every act of kindness;
for love will never stop loving.
No, it could never do that
because love knows

deep in its soul that
compassion wouldn't condone such an act.

"Therefore, I choose to show love above all else," said the Wise Man. "Love doesn't give a free ticket to do wrong, and it doesn't pretend the one doing wrong is not in error, but it does cover the offender with the hopes that they will see their mistake and make better choices. Actions motivated by love are never done with intentions to harm anyone but are done to help. Therefore, if I drew you in by any negative way from what I said earlier, I sincerely apologize. My comments were not meant to ignite the flames of uncontrollable curiosity in you. So, again, I repeat in love; I shall not share another person's business with you in this open forum, no matter how hungry you are to know it."

The Wise Man smiled kindly and segued into another thought. "Life is a big ball of beautiful and ugly realities that continuously unfold before us. Life is about choices timing and destiny, it's also about things we see and things we cannot."

"It's filled with cul-de-sacs and ditches that we can avoid because they're obvious. However, on the other side of the coin there are situations we would have avoided if we saw them coming, but that's not what destiny allowed. Destiny has delightful and hurtful realities which will take place whether we love or hate; whether we are kind or indifferent, whether we have forgotten our roots or maintained them in our advancements. That's just how it is," said the Wise Man, smiling. "Life presents things we can't sidestep, but the things we can, let's go around them; let's not get stuck in holes we have the power to avoid."

"I completely agree with you" interjected a tall, slender well-groomed man with a British accent. Then, chuckling, he said, "Life is funny" and paraphrased the Wise Man's words. "Things happen every day that we cannot avoid and there are things we would like to know, and we never will," he said, adding his personal thoughts.

"Thank you for those comments," said the Wise Man nodding his head in the Englishman's direction and continued sharing his views.

"When we began this journey together, I said to everyone, every road lead's somewhere, and our road will continue forward, so let's march on together. Let's not get bogged down debating issues we can't settle presently and let's stay on track.

There's more I'd like to share."

Looking directly at the Englishman with a respectful gaze, the Wise Man moved forward with a philosophical viewpoint.

God Blessed Life

The unexpected turns
and bends in the road of life
very rarely come with warning signs.
Health issues, marriage problems, and
wayward children
are never part of the plan
that we've designed for our life.
Human nature endeavors to bypass
each hurtful, testy, frustrating,
and stressful situation if possible.
Not that we don't like challenges,
we just don't like unplanned ones.
But there came a break in the road,
a dip you did not see, that subsequently
pushed your life in an unexpected direction,
a direction you would have never selected.
Therefore, you pondered life's strange timing.
But where pain and suffering appear,
comfort always resides.
In every problem, lives a solution.
Through struggles, inner strength is revealed.
Right across from sorrow, there is hope.
In poverty's neighborhood, there is provision.
Where sickness lives, healing dwells.
Thus, the bends, dips, and turns reveal a greater goodness
countering every evil, setback, ill, or obstacle

along the path of our life's journey.
So, even if life came with a roadmap
or high-tech GPS system
that charted the bumps, dips, and curves in the path,
inevitably, we would receive some scars,
some hurts, some bruises, and some losses.
For written into the DNA of humanity
are the unavoidable: jeopardy, calamity, and tragedy
which account for much of man's difficulties.
However, without these in a life intertwined,
man would not represent
a realistic presentation of the beautiful story
of a wonderfully God blessed life.

"Life will have its ups and downs; even the lofty and high-minded are not exempt from trouble. Problems certainly have a way of searching everyone out no matter where we go or who we are. Those that love and those that don't still face misfortune's grip. The wise and the foolish are challenged with difficulties. Humanity is like metal, and problems are like a magnet pulling each one of us into its grasp. Sometimes the struggles of life can feel like a spider's web," the Wise Man sighed and continued. "There's a ritual I've used over the years in which I ask God to assist me with each day—I merely pray."

Gain Through Loss

Father, help me today
to count my losses in struggles
not as losing more than I gain.
Remind me Lord
and help me to see,
you can develop my patience in a struggle,
give me more wisdom from a trial, and help me
gain a deeper regard for you through difficulties.
The strength to endure the next time I am challenged
by the loss of someone or something comes through the test.
So, Father I realize
that I may not be thoroughly prepared
for the next hardship that arises.
However, due to previous struggles
You've brought me through,
I will be better prepared to accept the loses,
and hold onto you in difficulties.
Father, I will walk with you today.
So, help me to see beyond every loss and behold the higher gain.

"Since some of the most hurtful experiences are the most helpful, we should let them be our teachers, our friends, so to say, not our enemies." He chuckled reflectively, glanced at someone or something that had briefly caught his attention and continued. "My mother would call all of us into the kitchen twice a year to give us cod liver oil. Boy, that was a nasty and hurtful experience, not to mention inflicted by someone I trusted and loved. It may not have been as bad as breaking a leg, having cancer, or something of that nature, but for me, it was a trying and sad experience."

"Anyway, my point is that cod liver oil and the grace of God kept us well through the years and gave our bodies a better constitution. I can't remember any of us getting sick. So, that unwanted experience had beneficial effects. I remember another painful lesson that had helped my brother and me. He loved climbing trees; some of you here can certainly relate to that." A few laughs were scattered throughout the audience. The faces summed up what they knew had happened. "Well, long story short, as you've already guessed, he fell and broke his arm. It could have been much worse."

"Nevertheless, that bad experience, that painful lesson, gave him a healthy respect for trees and a higher view of the value of life besides teaching him to be more careful in his adventures."

"I realize my examples were from two opposite ends of the spectrum," the Wise Man said chuckling.

"One experience was caused deliberately, and the other happened accidentally but both served a purpose; they proved that painful experiences can indeed work out for the good." Everyone seemed to be in agreement with his statements, so he progressed further with his thoughts.

"I believe, hurtful and trying experiences are beneficial because they test the true character of an individual. Some people's difficult experiences have made them calloused, and angry, bitter and cruel. Instead of the challenge or trouble creating a humble spirit in them, they become filled with pride and arrogance, or doubt, indifference, ingratitude, and animosity."

"Their character reminds me of a tale I once heard about a beautiful lioness in the plains of Africa. She was a very graceful and powerful lioness, but very full of conceit and self-importance. She would strut by the other lionesses with her head held in disdain for them. None of the lionesses could run as fast or hunt as well as her, she was the queen and boy, did she flaunt it. Well, as fate would have it, she received an injury to one of her legs. Oddly enough, no one knew what happened; she just came hobbling back to the pride injured yet attempting to continue her arrogant and pride filled ways."

"One day, when it was time for them to hunt again, this prideful and arrogant lioness wanting to once again assert her loftiness, attempted to take the lead and chase a huge zebra which she supposed would be easy pickings for her. That zebra kicked her several times in the face, which was quite embarrassing and painful, plus it was almost fatal! As the zebra trotted off to live another day, that lioness learned the very truthful lesson from the Wisdom of Solomon King of Israel. "Pride goes before destruction; and a haughty spirit before a fall, when pride comes, then comes shame; but with the lowly is wisdom" (KJV). Those were King Solomon's words, and that painful experience should have given her sobriety and snapped her out of her arrogant drunkenness."

"Nevertheless, it didn't, she just became more defensive, more aggressive, and even more prideful. Her pride and stubbornness eventually ruined her. That's what pride does; it closes our eyes to the beauty in humility. It makes us boastful and self-willed, calloused and hard-hearted. Hurtful experiences are a part of life! It is how we handle those experiences that makes a world of difference!"

"One last example," said the Wise Man. "Imagine the poison of a venomous snake bite, very hurtful and very damaging, yet that same venom is used as an antidote for snake bites. So, on one side, the experience may hurt, and on the flip side, that experience can help if we let it work as a positive, not a negative."

"That's my attitude now, being able to gain through loss. It took me a while to develop that posture but using the wisdom in humility instead of being prideful always makes us better."

He smiled, and his next words came forward as if he was thinking out loud, "wisdom is free, but using it is invaluable! And if we can agree that trouble comes to everyone's door, it seems to me that the world could use a few more laughs, a few more jokes and humor, fewer frowns and much more lightheartedness—that would help tremendously! People should spend more time being joyful!"

My friend Luana says this all the time, "Laugh! It doesn't cost a thing; Laughter truly is priceless." Luana looked at him and smiled. He laughed and playfully encouraged them with these words.

Smile!

A smile is free,
but what it's worth is priceless.
Coming from the heart,
a smile is nicest.
Giving a smile
is one way of showing
a gesture of friendship.
The expression of caring,
A smile is infectious,
spreads outward with ease
from somewhere inside us
each time we feel pleased.
It warms like the sunlight
anyone in its presence;
A face with no smile
has a somber existence.
A smile is quite vital,
it's healthy as humor.
A basic ingredient
to maintain youthful luster.
Far more essential than
fine gold which is
not quite comparable to
a smile's endless riches.

"Yes, a smile is quite valuable and very powerful," said the Wise Man smiling. "I'm certain everyone here can remember someone's smile that has had a great effect on you. Therefore, I strongly suggest that we all take time to smile because troubles, struggles and difficulties will not cease. So, hold onto a smile like you would hold onto love."

The sound of the door popping open echoed through the room as more people entered and some left. He grinned cheerfully and continued. "I'm sure you've discovered that the smile is the tattletale for our heart and sometimes for our mind. It's like the person that can't help but spill the beans when they are excited. The secrets that the heart holds, the smile reveals. It also uncovers our thoughts at times because they are in direct correlation to each other. Big tattletale," he said laughing and continued. "However, at times it seems like the smile, the mind, and the heart have individual personalities, and they're struggling to see who has the most power and warring to see who has the greatest authority."

"All three are very fascinating, all three can present facades, and as we know all three can extend beauty and comfort.

So, who has the most power—the smile, the mind or the heart? It's a great debate, but you decide for yourself. My conclusion is our hearts have the strongest persuasion, especially when it is overwhelmed with emotion."

The Wise Man shifted on the stool again, scratched his head and continued. "Our hearts can be like smart dictators, whispering orders to our souls, minds, and our faces. Sometimes they seem like an individual entity within us, something like a world within a world that pulls at us from so many directions." He paused, then tilted his head to a strange angle that looked oddly uncomfortable, then shook it back into a horizontal position and continued onward.

"The heart is a vast land of emotions, will, and desires which have a determination and a spectrum so broad in range and depth that it would take more than a few lifetimes to know it entirely. We laugh! We cry! We frown! We smile! And we all naturally pursue someone's heart which causes us to smile or frown. I guess it's built within us to want to get to know that great land of mystery more thoroughly," he continued his thoughts with passion.

Affection

The human heart is quite mysterious;
it yields itself like a servant
and demands honor like a king or queen.
It can be humble or proud, generous, or stingy.
It can love or hate, give itself entirely or partially.
It is a fortress with soldiers watching at the gates,
a brazen city not easily besieged,
but always capable of being captured.
Who can take it captive?
Who can possess its treasures?
He that can persuade the maidens to gander
or
she who can woo the soldiers to surrender
that the footmen crossover without a battle,
and the gentry without a controversy.,
There will be no need for weapons
when the drawbridge has been lowered.
The petitioner can proceed with affection
as the pledge of surrender and commitment,
then graciously present their declaration
as an offering of assurance.
So, the gates are opened for noblemen,
and the gates are open for princes.
The hoary head and the nursing child,
The strong and the feeble,
The courageous and the coward,

are all welcome in the castle.
The damsels do enter and male servants,
paupers and beggars are allowed on the red carpet
for the nobleman and the pauper are the same.
The prince, the damsel, and the beggar
are of the same blood.
Night and day, the chambers are opened,
day and night the bed is ready
with love waiting to be surrendered,
and love waiting to be captured,
and love extending love again
with the lowly demeanor of a servant,
but, with the soul of a king or a queen,
the heart is quite mysterious.

"Oh, the heart," he said, "the mysterious heart!" He nodded his head slowly, got up from the stool and took out the reading glasses he had in his pocket. From another pocket, he pulled out a folded piece of paper. Delicately, like a cardiologist performing surgery, he unfolded the paper and perused its content with a smile of endearment.

He sat down again and made himself comfortable. He put the glasses and the paper back in his pockets, looked around the room a few times, and continued to share his observations of the heart. "Truly mysterious! Yes, genuinely mysterious the heart is, and love is one of the fascinating things that live in it." He looked directly at his lovely wife and shared his intimate thoughts with her as we all listened carefully.

You

If I were Shakespeare, I'd write of you and compare you to a rose,
the rising sun, the full moon of early spring,
the glittering of the stars and the grace and beauty of a peacock.
If I were Beethoven, I'd pen you as a concerto and lovingly describe you in each note.
I'd flute your voice, piano your smile, violin your movements, drum roll your steps, and bass your body.
Your eyes would be the clashing of the symbols each time you flashed them closed and opened.
If I were Michelangelo,
I'd spend my life in capturing all images from all angles of you on all mediums and
I'd blush your face with shades of pink, accent your hair with hues in brown, and
lounge you in pastels from the rainbow.
I'd mellow you in yellow, sink you in pink, and warm you in lavender.
If I were Miles Davis and feeling kind of blue,
I'd gather Nat and Cannonball Adderley,
John Coltrane, and Joe Zawinul to swing while I exclaim
my appreciation of you with mercy-mercy-mercy,
what a love supreme.
If I were a melody and words to a song,
I'd want to be sung and played only by you.

If I were a poem, I'd want to be written by Paul Laurence Dunbar and recited by Fredrick Douglas to only you.
If I were GOD, Yes, GOD, I'd make you merely you.

In almost perfect harmony, the crowd turned in the direction of the Wise Man's wife. Blushing softly, her eyes beamed with radiance as she looked at her husband. As if reading the minds of everyone in the room, the Wise Man again spoke, "Oh, sweet love! Love an adjective, love a noun, and love a verb! It is ever-present around us while it grows within us! Oh, dearest love of my heart, you are my sunshine when the clouds are gray. And I know sweetheart that I am happier because of you and the life we share together then I could ever be journeying through this life without you." The Wise Man sounded like one of the early poets, but he didn't seem to care. He plowed forward with another romantic overture when he affectionately stated ...

Just Because

Some send chocolates, flowers, even diamonds as gifts
to make up after an argument.
A fight.
A mistake.
Some do it to ask for forgiveness
for an unfaithful act in the relationship.
Some because it's Christmas, a birthday, or
because of an anniversary.
Some ask will you be mine because it's Valentine's Day.
Some even do it with an ulterior motive,
expecting much more in return than what they ever give.
I, too, have a because,
just because I love you,
just because I care,
just because you deserve it and because you are you.

There was a deep warmth in his demeanor as he declared the depth of his love for her. The onlookers were drawn into the beauty of their years together; it was all revealed in that interval of time when they gazed at each other. The sweet intimacy of their connection, and the intensity of their gaze was a real panacea; medication for hurts and pains that pharmacist would love to have owned and bottled. The Wise Man paused for a few moments as he and his wife continued to embrace each other with their gaze. When he spoke again, his words squeezed us firm and gentle like when one's breath is taken away by delightful surprise.

Along the Way

At the altar of the new frontier
I recalled us traversing through
the vast plains of friendship
and sailing through diverse seas of emotion
endeavoring to build a stable relationship.
I remembered the days of walking through
the sandy deserts of misunderstanding,
thirsting for the water of restoration.
In the itchy sweet grass of courtship,
we played like children, and there we grew,
developing our strengths and accepting our weaknesses
as we moved along the way.
I recall that endearing moment
when we both discovered
that being still can be enough
to bring forward progress
and broaden the horizons of our understanding
for each other.
How exciting it was to experience
Our hearts being entwined together
as we ventured along the way towards our new frontier.
What a soul-stirring delight I saw captured in your eyes,
your smile reflecting, and projecting
what was present in your heart.
My smile was thanking you for the beautiful discovery
that the journey's end indeed is not the highest goal

but, experiencing every salty or savory detail
along the way is.
I do. I will. Forever!

Giving his dear lady one more affectionate embrace with his eyes as if he were proposing to her again, he tenderly said, "Many years ago, I spoke those words and my heart, and my soul still says yes. Each moment we share together is a precious moment well spent. You're like blood in my veins and a symphony in my thoughts and every day with you I realize …

Love

I can hear love whispering in the breeze
I can feel love in the warmth of the sunrays
I can see love in the budding of the trees
I can touch love in the light of the moon
I can smell love in the fragrance of the flowers
I can enjoy love in the lap of nature
For I'm touched and blessed with the love of God

And you are that precious gift he gave me.
"My dear, you are like love from God.
The very love of God which surpasses mere emotion!"

Part III

CHANGING
THE
BRUSH

"Good relationships aren't always easy to develop or maintain" said the Wise Man smiling, "but I'm sure most of you have already discovered that if you've been in a relationship for a substantial amount of time. It's always a give-and-take, and it's not about fifty-fifty. Some days, you'll have to give ninety-nine, and all your mate can provide is one, and that one is their 100 on that day. It works both ways," said the Wise Man thoughtfully. "However, when we want the best relationship possible, we work at it every day."

"Let me give you an example. Two people got married, they were extremely happy. Twice a day they would call each other or send a text, just to say, 'Hi, just checking to see how your day is going.' They sent little funny emojis that said I love you! They were obviously in love. Every moment felt like a fresh spring day. Then, summer came, and things were still going well. He had a reasonably good paying job; she was at home taking care of the household and family. Four children can be expensive, so he took a part-time job for extra income. He wanted to make sure they always had more than enough."

"Autumn came and they had advanced fairly well financially, and everything seemed to be stable, yet in all their personal endeavors, advancements, and interests in being achievers, and wanting to take care of the kids and make the right impression on others, they hadn't paid close enough attention to each other. They were growing but not together! His mind was on making sure he could continue to be the great provider for the family. Her mind was on being the perfect person—perfect mom, perfect friend, perfect hostess, perfect mother. They were putting a lot of pressure on themselves, and on each other. and they had lost the tender compassion they once shared. Deep down inside they realized there was an underlying problem, but they never truly dealt with their giants. They attempted to put band aids on their emptiness, through work, the kids, and routines."

"They tried talking but they had become fault finders. They were engaged in the blame game and had become selfish and unyielding. Some days, they were so impatient with each other, that the slightest thing caused an eruption or a gross misunderstanding. They had lost their ability to see the beauty in each other. The beauty in the simple things they shared as a couple in the spring and summer of their relationship were forgotten also. Their conversation had changed, their communication broke down, and so their demeanor and perspective of each other changed as well. Autumn had shaken them, and winter's complexity had grabbed them. They still loved each other, though not unconditionally."

"Unconditional love is essential, and simplicity is always grand in relationships because it is never the big thing that causes the most problems. It's a compilation of small things which aren't properly dealt with or tended to that causes the dam to overflow. It's forgetting to be sensitive to your partner's needs. It's forgetting that neither of you are perfect nor do you have to be. Sometimes there are things built up in couples that they don't even realize are affecting them, and the pinch of those unseen things will come out in strange ways and at strange times."

"That's why I say to every couple—don't put pressure on yourself to be perfect or to have perfect children, or to keep up with society's standard of what success is. Make it your objective to love each other unconditionally, to forgive continuously, and to always be content with each other! Look at each issue together and find a way in it where you can agree, in love. Don't ever let your will, material advancement, or the children be your central focus; make each other the priority. The marriage must have the top shelf."

He waited, allowing his words to grab everyone and continued. "I am always reminded of the difference between being "in love" and loving someone as God loves. "In love" can relate to the emotional high the feelings give us. Loving unconditionally, however, is a choice that is made. It's a person choosing to love someone in spite of everything. It's loving them every day, with all their flaws and failures; without trying to force them into what we want them to be. There are no days off when we choose to love each other in that way."

"One last thing, though the most important point of all. Put Christ first in your marriage because marriage is a covenant with Him and each other. Seek His advice, follow His instructions, obey His commands and your marriage will be successful. It's God's promise to you as a couple. Some of you here may believe you don't need God's help to manage your marriage or your family. I won't argue with you, but I will share this following information. No matter how strong you believe your relationships are, they can be 100 times better with Christ's leadership."

"Therefore, I repeat lovingly to each couple here with families, or planning to have one, let Christ lead you in your relationships. He'll give you everything you need to have the best connection possible. He'll show you how to love unconditionally, and the journey will be wonderful. I say this from the depth of my soul and bottom of my heart."

The Wise Man stood and shook his legs to stretch them, walked a few feet from the stool and asked if someone could bring him a chair. Two young men carried the chair and sat it near him, "thank you," he said, addressing them simultaneously. They replied, "you're welcome" and walked away. The Wise Man took a couple sips of water, positioned himself more comfortably in the chair and made a request. "Men I have something I would like to ask you all to consider. However, before I share it, I do admit that for some of you it may seem a bit unnecessary and for others, it may seem a bit pushy. Some of you guys may think to yourselves, "I'm doing that now" but in any case, it's my request, and I'm asking each of you to …

Be (To Every Man)

Be as loyal as a dog
Be as cautious as a cat
Be as wise as an owl
As tenacious as a gnat
Be as clever as a fox
As playful as a monkey
Be persistent as an ant
Be unmovable as a donkey
Be as gentle as a dove
Be as courageous as a lion
Be as watchful as a hawk
Be able to blend like a chameleon
Be family oriented like the quails
Be enduring like a camel
Take your time like the snails
But soar high like an eagle.
Don't live in the past
and seriously consider the future
and besides all of this
there's one more important feature.
In all your dealings in life
the principle thing to understand
is to work on your character daily
and always be a humble man.

"I realize these are challenging words, but the challenge is simple. I'm challenging every man to keep the determination and dedication to practice what is meaningful, purposeful, and valuable, and to remain humble on the mountain top and in the valley."

"I sincerely believe that family, society, one's self, and the future is connected to all three and therefore, they should be highly significant to any man. That's why I aim my arrows high and shoot at the target every day. For any day I can fall miserably short as a man and become proud and boastful. But, believe me, I am grappling with myself each day to be the best I can.

I once met a man who was one of the most excellent examples of down to earth manhood that I have ever known." He shifted slightly in his chair and continued speaking.

He Painted the Wind!

Standing about 6'4" to 6'6" at the shoulders, his body seemed to have been chiseled from pure ebony and lovingly polished to a smooth, flawless finish.

He appeared to be one muscle with the features of a man.

I encountered or should I say I "experienced" him on the beach in Venice California.

While strolling on the crowded walkway, I was startled by a rushing sound that was thumping on sand that had blown up on the sidewalk.

As I turned to see what was causing that sound, I saw the Wind painter.

He was painting the wind as he effortlessly seemed to float on rollerblades. He sliced, twisted, turned, weaved and moved in and out of the crowd like a flag flowing in the breeze.

Like an artist dipping his brush in lamp black and streaking it across a canvas, his motions painted the wind. His skin-tight, pale blue t-shirt flowed in harmony with his navy-blue spandex athletic pants. A long pale blue scarf draped over his shoulder floated, danced and flowed in a hypnotic motion with each weave in or out left or right movement. He seemed to leave black and blue spinning, swirling designs on the wind.

I watched him in total amazement as he danced and floated effortlessly through the crowd.

I continued my stroll westward until I arrived at the area of the old roller coaster where he and a group of skaters, male and female, dressed in hot pink, bright green, yellow and red clothing skated. They also moved with ease and speed weaving in and out of about 100 orange cones placed in a straight line. After each run through the cones, the skaters would gather around the wind painter who seemed to choreograph each move.

Music was added, and one by one, more color was added to the canvas, they moved in syncopation with the music as if a breeze had gently lifted them and put them in motion.

The wind painter and an attractive female approached the mouth of the cones; he was the notes, she was the melody. As they moved in perfect harmony, he drifted to the right side of the cones, and she floated to the left side with the precise movement and perfect timing of a Swiss watch. They turned, faced each other, and gracefully their movement changed with the tempo of the music. They met at the face of the cone line, ebony, navy blue and pale blue moved to the left and ivory, hot pink and yellow moved to the right. Then, holding hands as they skated, she arched her back and leaned back towards the top of the cones. Her body encircled the cones to the left as he skated to the right, the colors streaked and swirled in and out and up and down in one smooth action. Like steam rising upward on a cold crisp day, her body rose to a standing position and coupled to his body as one. Her head rested on his chest, and her long platinum hair hung like a tassel that was attached to it. They returned to the top of the line painting something like that resembling a Leroy Neiman painting on the wind.

He was a great man. I learned that over the years and came to regard him as one of my dearest friends and confidants. He had great character, and it was he that inspired some of the thoughts that I've shared with you today. He was also a great friend, a good father, a brilliant thinker and just one heck of a great dude! He passed away some years ago, but I am indeed grateful for the friendship we had and the camaraderie we shared. He introduced me to my sweetheart, and that was one of the most beautiful moments of my life. The day I met my sweet lady enhanced my views in so many ways, and his friendship and integrity has influenced me just as much.

I would be hard pressed to tell you about my life's experiences without mentioning these two superstars.

The crowd began to applaud. He waited until the applause ceased and said, "you don't find many men like him. Devoted men that are strong and gentle and have learned the balance of work and play, that have learned how to make a living and live." Everyone was nodding their head like bobblehead dolls in a car window. "That's why I applaud men like that. Do you realize how many men are devoted to everything but the most important things?

Often, we men think that making money is making a living and that if we are good financial providers that we have done our duty. Sometimes we mistake being physically present in the house with being mentally present in the home. So, let me throw this out there gently—many men are missing although they are seen in the house. Think about this.

Missing While Being There

In every state of this great nation
many men are missing
much of the most vital segments
of their family's lives.
These are not deadbeat dads
that show no concern for their families.
These men cherish their wives.
These men love their children.
These are good men and
hardworking providers.
They are not reclining in a La-Z—boy,
being a lazy man, or
wasting their substance on foolishness.
Nevertheless, these fathers are absent.
And these fathers are missing—
missing their sons and daughter's activities,
missing their sons and daughter's development,
missing their wife's deeper feelings, and
missing their family's best years!
They're eagerly scratching it out to make a living,
but missing the opportunities to live.
Slow down! Take a moment to reflect! Take a break!
Take the time to enjoy your family!
Turn the phone off!
Put the studies away!
Cancel the appointments!

Get away from work!
Make some time to enjoy your lives.
I am confident it will enhance yours
and the entire household will reap significant benefits.
Making a living must stay in proportion with living
or the entire family structure will be continuously
missing balance.
Some of the men were a bit irritated with the Wise Man's statements and voiced their opinions without hesitation.

"I'm doing the best I can and that's good enough for me," said one man, staring at the Wise Man intently. Another muscular- looking guy standing near him said, "When you provide for my household then we can talk." "You think we don't want to stay home with our families? added a few others as they chimed in, voicing their irritation. The atmosphere had shifted but the Wise Man was keenly aware that his comments would probably push some buttons or raise some eyebrows. Nevertheless, he was determined to share his experiences and his views in candid honesty with the hope that his words would be a bridge that men would walk across to get to a place of better. He wasn't trying to build a wall, but even at the cost of irritating or losing a few listeners, he had decided to speak his mind in love. He then humbly declared…

I Am That Man

I am that man
who in a moment of time
beyond the brink, may not think
exactly like you, and inadvertently may offend you.
And it may send you
a negative impression
but that does not entirely reveal or steal
from whom I am.
For I love dearly, hurt severely,
can pretend
sometimes, and sometimes not, but then
I do remember, clearly do remember
and I have not forgotten ...
that pain hurts, and love, basically feels good.
And I would
love to see the day when joy and pain decide
no longer to reside side by side.
I am that man
That has loved and hated, and
anticipated so many things
that never came.
Been called a genius
but I still felt lame.
I tried to stand, and I failed, dug in
but couldn't bail me out.
Doubt has often plagued me,

faith has always lifted me,
God has truly gifted me with much,
And still
I find time to shout
and then humorously laugh about
the man I am.
I am that man
who joyously lives,
and generously gives
what I have without resentment.
To the one that does pretend
with all sincerity to be a friend
while being used as evil's instrument.
But I smile, and they smile,
then we smile at the same time
but not for the same reasons.
For I know all things within their seasons
will be revealed.
And not being oversensitive
nor insensitive, I sense you feel
a particular uncertainty about me
but alas, I must be real.
I am that man
that passionately into life springs
and through it all sings
I hope this technique works,
and in the presence of all the jerks
that long to see me splatter.
If I crash, their thoughts won't matter
to a dead man!
So, if just before the crash,
I see my whole life flash

in amazingly beautiful graphics.
My life,
small or astronomical,
severely serious or purely comical,
like the classics
that are hard to understand
represent the total package
of whom I am;
I am the man that I am.

"So please understand, I am not trying to offend anyone, but if by chance I do, don't take it personally, we're not trying to make this a glass house experience or a stone-throwing contest.

I am certain that all of you love your families, but there is always room for improvement. I believe that any man who wants the best for his family should be willing to listen to advice. It's your choice if you want to use it or not. Ruth Harvey (2005), put it this way: 'A man is known by his... Character—what he is. Conversation—-what he says. Conduct—-what he does. Contribution—-what he gives. Creed—-what he believes.'" (pg. 51)

"Therefore, I suggest we move forward, for life is too short to get hung up and set back by things that offend us. We must learn to move ahead and press towards better at all times. As men we must strive for greater things and never allow our egos, or pride to hold us in bondage. So, let's move forward, gentlemen. "

He smiled warmly, and that effortless smile covered his face again. His genuine true spirit seemed to circle the room and engulf each listener with the natural clarity of what he meant. Surely, there was no reason to be touchy and sensitive over the issues that the Wise Man shared. He was not targeting anyone specifically. He was merely sharing his life, stating his discoveries, and expressing his views. For the most part, everyone had moved on. The few that dallied behind in pity or anger were gradually acquiescing into what he was then saying, as he segued gently, returning to his past to make a point.

Down by the Stream

As a child, my favorite play area was down by the stream
that flowed in the shadow of a majestic big red barn.
I remember wading in its crisp, fresh water in the spring,
and listening to the cries of animals and chirping birds.
I enjoyed the flowers that filled the air with fragrances
so sweet that it seemed to intoxicate me.
When the summers were hot, I would lie in the rushing waters
for what seemed to be endless hours.
I'd bundle up in the winter, slip and slide on the ice
until I was exhausted.
I'd rush home soaked clear through, my mom would scold,
bathe, and hug me, and then send me to bed,
but sleep was always slow to come.
I must have fallen asleep for a very long time …
Yesterday I went to my favorite spot
and was astonished by the reflection in the stream.
There before me was an age I had not witnessed.
There was wisdom in the voice of time that spoke to me
saying, "Fear not what you see, be as you were
when you did not see with those eyes!
See where you were and not where you are,"
I replied "Rustic is the barn, wrinkled is the skin,
tattered and torn is the roof, broken is the glass,
gray the hair, some missing, weak are the eyes.
The loft and rafters are weak and broken, the hands, back,
and knees are sore, sometimes bent and stooped.

So how can I be as I was?
The voice of time seemed to find humor in that and said, "My son! Did you not smile and find joy and happiness here?"

"Joy and happiness," the Wise Man said reflectively, "are very important things. And throughout my journeys, I have discovered some things affect us in strange ways and can throw us off balance, stealing our joy and contentment. Therefore, we must learn to return to the source that brings peace in us because life is always moving forward. Life does not stop for us because we are disgruntled or in disagreement with someone or something. I have come to this conclusion he said very seriously: life gives us the choice of flowing with it or fighting with it. And believe me, fighting it is hard, especially when it is unnecessary. Furthermore, being disgruntled also burns a lot of pointless energy."

"Therefore, whenever I feel frustration's grip trying to get the better of me or I become sensitive because of what someone said or did, I take myself back down by the stream where I find peace again. I remind myself of the freedom in youthfulness and the refreshment of being a child. More specifically, I remind myself I am a child of the King. And I don't have to go around being offended! You can do the same if you trust Him too. So, bear with me during the rough spots as we take these bumps in the road together. I'm just doing my best to share insights that I have gathered over the years, which is the very reason we are here today."

"I pray these insights will challenge everyone here to reach for better throughout your home and all other aspects of your journey. Hopefully, these suggestions will be a source of encouragement for you, your family and friends. The changes, and choices we make will always affect us, the people around us, and the following generation."

The Wise Man smiled, cleared his throat and continued. "There is a system to life and a time for all things good and bad. If we allow offenses to control us, we may miss the beauty presented in the next moment. And in that brief progression of time, a new season could begin which could impact our life significantly. We don't want to miss it! So, be alert, be strong and be encouraged. Embrace the things that challenge you because no one can control the seasons or the next moment.

The most important thing anyone needs to control is themselves!

In the Season

The seasons roll according to their time.
Who may dictate to them when to come or go?
No farmer plants out of season and expects to reap a harvest.
No one, by his own will or strength, can tell the rain to fall
or stop the wind from blowing.
No man can produce a life of his own doing;
it comes within its season.
No person can alter the world's rotation to meet their demands.
Our lives are framed within seasons and our strength is greatest within its season.
Life moves us in the direction of the new season.
We may fight, struggle, and try to manipulate life
but the seasons come when they come,
and no man's will can prevail against them.
We can achieve what is possible in that season.
For every season brings with it everything attached to it.
Seasons do not slow down waiting for us.
Even if a season lasts longer than usual, it will have an end.
Don't miss your season;
your highest potential is connected to it and
your most significant power is developed in it.
The best in you is grown out of it.
Your destiny meets you there
in the season!

"Seasons," said the Wise Man, "are so essential because they give us a picture of the necessity of using time wisely as life continues to change. There is the sad reality of people wasting valuable time, precious moments that will never come back. So, we must learn to develop within the seasons, keeping an open mind, heart, and spirit not to miss what's offered in that time frame for change and development."

"God has placed the possibility of better in worse-case scenarios.
There is always something good to be found if we are willing to look for it."
"Simply put, what I have gathered from life is that God holds power over every season, and he declares how long they will last and the struggles that we will face in them.

He gives us guidelines and attaches consequences to our decisions. All people have the same chances with God because He is never prejudice, or unfair. He can see every heart and the desires and intentions in it. He knows what's best for everyone, and He wants us to live every day full of love, joy and peace because He wants us to trust him. Therefore, trusting God," said the Wise Man, "makes every season fruitful, even in the times of famine."

He rubbed his hands together once again with a motion that seemed very similar to that of washing one's hands. Appearing to have invisible soap and water that only he could see, he continued the action a few more seconds. Then, he placed his freshly washed hands on his lap, one on each leg and moved them from his inner thigh almost to the knee a few times as if to dry them. Once the drying motion stopped, he crossed his arms over his chest and gave this neologism.

All About Breath

Just for a few moments allow me to suggest
considering life not in seconds, days, months, or years
but as having an allotment of breaths.
Would you live your life in trivia and insignificance?
Or would it be your goal to use each breath wisely
and thereby make a world of difference?
Where are you taking your breath today?
And where is your breath taking you?
And what with your breath today, may I inquire,
are you planning to do?
Will it assist someone in conquering a problem
or will your breath be their noose?
Since breath is the main element in every stage of life,
how will you put yours to use?
Will your breath be a hindrance,
a block in someone's life, an obstacle in someone's path
or will your breath produce treasures that last?
Will your breath be uplifting, encouraging or positive?
Or will it be mingled and mixed with insults,
among other abusive negatives?
Do you lend your breath to misdirection,
yield it to profanity, allow it to dabble in vile affections,
slur it with alcohol's intoxication,
Alter it with drugs and their breath-changing dictation?
Or, do you gag it with good old tobacco smoke,
the addictive substance that is now labeled "dope"?

How much breath do you use for exercise?
How much breath do you use to criticize?
How much breath is used to hurt?
How much breath is used for work?
How much breath is used for you,
for acquaintances, loved ones, or friends?
How much of God's freely given air
have we gratefully or selfishly breathed in?
Consider this simple poem
and sincerely treasure each breath,
for every breath is linked to life
and each one is next to death.
And having the breath to hear this poem
means mercy has been your friend.
Thus, each breath should be used wisely
for on each breath, your life does hinge.

"Our lives are hanging on a breath he said, a breath that is not guaranteed; breath that we often take for granted, breath that is a gift from God! Yes, each day that we wake up, God blesses us with the ability to inhale and exhale. Hmm…He breathed in and out as if to take in thoroughly and breathe out completely the brevity of his own words. He continued, "if we could only see it that way maybe things would be different because we would recognize the value of the air that we are sharing with each other, in every moment, every day and every season."

"I honestly don't think we would be hung up on petty things if we genuinely considered life is in each breath." He looked at his first-born child who was attending the gathering and chuckled. He gazed at her endearingly and said, "I vividly remember your first breath and that beginning of a new season."

The Birthday

After nine months of anticipation,
beholding you
so tiny, so comely, so fragile;
immediately,
I loved you.
Thoughts became realities;
responsibility
stared me straight in the face.
Looking back,
my heart remembered
every concern,
every prayer,
every promise.
Suddenly,
there you were—
the beautiful continuance of life.
They handed you to your mother,
and
in turn to me.
Unconsciously,
I had given you me long ago ...
the moment your mother said,
"I'm pregnant."
A few days after your birthday,
we left the hospital
together,

a golden, radiant day.
Lord, life sure smells good!

Those were the words I uttered after I buckled you in the car seat. Life sure smells good! Breath! Yes, wonderful breath! And from breath to breath you grew beautifully. And as time sped by, suddenly you were no longer a child but a young woman full of radiance and heading in your adult direction." He glanced at her again and shared these …

Reflections

My daughter crossed my mind in astounding sound and video.
I recalled her questions and statements far beyond her years
which made me laugh or grind my teeth,
but always prompted consideration.
Some days she was light flashing across a midnight sky,
then autumn rains landing so effortlessly on my heart
that powder snow or the promise of spring,
couldn't compare to those little girl grown-up ways.
Those little girl grown-up ways pulled at me with invisible
strings and persuaded me to be more than just a father.
They compelled me to be a daddy made not of glass,
but to be a dad transparent as glass in our interactions.
A daddy! A father! Not understanding everything,
but doing everything to be fully understanding.
I reflected as the sound reverberated.
Those passing years filled with challenges were fertilizer for both of us.
There were many times I held my breath
and whispered silent prayers.
The day she rested her dolls on the dresser top
and decided to try on clothes that made my mind say no,
and my mouth confrontational was evidence she was changing.
The princess that played with dolls was now a young lady,
more beautiful than Barbie.
The adolescent who said boys were silly
was now acting silly with boys.

"Living Kens!" that I eyeballed with fatherly scrutiny and attempted to watch like a hawk.
Oh, the fields she ran through, the plains, the valleys, and hills. Oh, the puddles she jumped in
and the mud she got on her clothes while testing,
and even challenging my boundaries with subtle confrontations. And while I smiled with parental concern,
and chastised her without condemnation, my heart would sometimes tremble, and butterflies lived in my stomach.
As I watched my daughter transition from childhood,
to womanhood daily; In the back of my mind,
there was this knowledge that pricked me now and then.
That suddenly the day would come, without drum rolls, without presentations or parades, and her fully developed wings would land her on a branch of her own. Leaving me the privilege of carrying these memories of struggles, challenges, and growth displayed in animated brightness and intensity. These would be my continuous treasures!
Endearing, vociferous recollections dialoguing in my thoughts without shadows. Vast pictures and voices echoing brilliantly and lingering in the halls of my mind while encouraging me, to remember that I helped her get wings.

It was evident his heart was overwhelmed with pride and thankfulness at how well she had developed and matured. It could not have been more obviously displayed on his face even if he had had a high-definition neon light flashing that said, "I'm proud of you, my child." The Wise Man's eyes were warm with emotion, not teary-eyed emotion, but that look that arises from a man's soul when he has experienced something more grandiose than the Niagara Falls or the Grand Canyon. For a few moments, the Wise Man was silent

... he took in a few quiet breaths, gathered his thoughts and with fatherly concern, continued expressing his sentiments.

"I believe that children are basically products of their environment; environments that they have been placed into, thrown into, forced into, or just born into. Their parents, peer pressure, circumstance or situation is what motivates them. Often, they feel pushed into action, and many times, their decisions are based on the weight on them at that moment. They react to what others in their peer group expect of them or in radical ways that make them feel they have control."

The Wise Man paused to reflect and continued. "In my opinion, a principle of finding the root or core issue of a child's behavior is watching the pattern of activity acted out from the source of stimulus received, and after a time of observation, the behavior pattern could reveal what is the problem. Most children have a certain pattern and even if their habits are subject to change because of their age or stage of development, they will act a certain way when threatened or if they feel insecure or uncertain; they will conduct themselves according to that feeling."

"It is basically because they don't know exactly who they are, where they're going, how to get to their destination, or how they fit into the great puzzle of life. Also, many of them do not understand the overall consequences of their actions when they do something devastating. It is in the best interests of the parent or caretaker involved with children to watch these patterns as they develop and work from this position of observation, as a point of how to best handle each situation as they surface."

The Wise Man waited for any comments or thoughts, shifted his gaze to a young couple with three children and continued. "There are no bad children. However, there are many misguided, misinformed, mistreated, abused, confused, and disappointed children. Some children have done cruel and evil things because of a lack of guidance or misguidance. Bullied children sometimes act out their hurt on other children. Children left to fend for themselves can become calloused. Some children have become manipulative or sneaky because of things that have happened in their lives or because of the bad examples that are before them, however, generally speaking, in my opinion, children are not evil; they are simply products of their environment."

The Wise Man shifted his gaze from the couple and continued talking. "Some children's life experiences have not been favorable. So, they operate from the standpoint of their hurt and disappointment because they don't know how to make the adjustments to handle their blows. And, if they don't know how to share those hurts with their parents or another adult, they can trust to help them, their viewpoint gets distorted, and pain and mistrust are often what they associate with life."

"From their distorted viewpoint, they act out in anger, aggression, frustration and other ways which display their off-centered perspective. Yes, it is a plea for affection, understanding, or help. However, this plea can be misinterpreted by the parent, caretaker or society which sees the act and not the frustration."

"One of the things I believe helps in these situations," said the Wise Man smiling, "is to allow the child a moment to vent, then talk to them about their emotions and how to better deal with those feelings. With your responses and actions, demonstrate how to handle situations and simmer down. Your demeanor and attitude will show them that calmness always beats having uncontrolled anger or being overly aggressive and that there is still a way to defuse bombs."

The Wise Man rubbed the corner of his left eye as if to get something out of it and continued. "Sometimes when a child acts disrespectful or disobedient, it is a signal that they are struggling with boundaries; they are trying to find themselves within the rules. At times, it may also mean that they have lost the clear line of what is expected of them or that they are struggling with how to handle a situation with their peers. They may be seeking security in the guidelines to be reestablished and the boundaries put back in place. Sometimes their battle is how to handle parental or adult authority and the changes in themselves. And, occasionally, a child is just testing the waters to see if you will bend and move your boundary line. Whatever the case, remind them that the rules you have set up are established because you care about them and you want the best for them; it's not because you want to keep them from enjoying their lives or becoming their own person."

"When discipline is necessary, do not restrain from it. I believe it is always important to gently yet firmly bring children back in bounds by reminding them of your instructions and enforcing some form of correction. As a parent or person caring for children, we must demonstrate that obedience and respect for rules indeed has its benefits, and violating those rules has consequences." The Wise Man glanced around the room again and looked up towards the ceiling as if he was looking at a thought hanging in that realm. He lowered his head and continued sharing.

"Interaction with youth is very significant, especially in their teenage years. The hurdle is getting them to communicate in transparency beyond the murky waters of their fears. How is this performed, you ask" said the Wise Man. "My first suggestion is always discussing issues that are important to them, then proceed into the other topics that are pertinent to the problems at hand. This way, they will feel more comfortable about opening up to the subjects that will aid their development into becoming more mature and more responsible in each juncture of their lives."

"Try not to take a child's actions personally, no matter how directly their actions affect you. They have not mastered the lessons of tactfulness or self-control in the areas where they feel overwhelmed. Some children can act like monsters, but basically, they are just unsure. So, sometimes their words will come out of their head, not their hearts. Remember, they are all too often stumbling around desperately trying to contain or express their feelings of frustration, pain, anger, etc.; they have not learned to act like an adult. Since we are the parents, the adults, and the teachers, we must remember that we were once young ourselves. Our words and actions weren't always noble when we were their age. Do your best to retain your self-control even when they fly off the handle. Gas doesn't put out fires! One last thing," said the Wise Man holding his hands together as if he was about to pray …

Influence

Be careful what you call your children;
your words have much power.
Inside every child is a seed growing
that will someday become a weed or a flower.
Words bring courage, fear, faith, doubt, love, hate,
joy or the opposite—sorrow.
And, there is this enormous possibility
that which is spoken to them today
could have control
of their lives tomorrow.
Words spoken can never be retrieved;
they don't just dissipate because you apologized.
It's those negative words
that have scarred many children for life
far more severely
then the hands which brutalized
them physically and left their bodies battered.
It's those words that blew their hopes away
and left them completely tattered.
And, often what was said to them,
those negative words and phrases,
are sadly practiced in detail
on the next generation of children.
This cycle could continue indefinitely,
but this cycle may be broken
by anyone wise enough to be cautious

of what they call their children.
Be careful what you call your children today;
your words have much power.
Inside your child is a seed growing
that will someday become a weed or a flower.

Continuing his chain of thought, in that same mellifluous tone to buffer any possible kickback from those who may have misunderstood his words for accusations of poor parenting, he said …

Guidance

The future is in our children;
they're our tomorrow, today.
So, we have to build them up
as they journey on their way.
We are the cheerleaders. We are the encouragers.
We discipline them. We are the enforcers.
We are the ladders that they should be able to climb on.
We are the foundation that they should be able to build on.
They're not going to get everything right.
They will certainly make some mistakes.
But, if we can teach them how to endure,
they won't succumb to life's bad breaks.
They won't buckle when they make an error,
but they'll chuckle in the face of dismay.
Not because they think to err is funny,
but because they'll know there's another day.
The foundation of the child is good for strength
when it's traversing through life's labyrinth.
As it travels over the hills and through the plains,
it will be learning from life's setbacks and life's gains—
how to take a seat and take a stand,
how to be secure and very stable,
how to accept the times when they're not able.
to accomplish all the things that life demands.
So, if the children are the continuation of our teachings
and the future is being built in them today,

we'd better make sure it's them we're reaching
and give them every aid along the way.

The Wise Man looked around the room once more and rubbed his hands together in a hand-washing motion. This seemed to be a form of finality, as if this motion or gesture was his body language for saying, "I pray you'll accept in good faith what I've just shared with you." He chuckled and in a light-hearted way, verbally stated what his body language revealed. Then, he said very seriously, "Every child is special and wonderfully unique" and as James Baldwin put it, and I quote, "These are all our children, and we will either pay for or profit from whatever they become" (n.d.).

The Wise Man chuckled once more, turned slightly, and moved to his right. "Time rushes by so quickly that we must really make good use of our time! Yesterday she was a sweet innocent curly-haired baby, he glanced in his daughter's direction once more, and today she's a beautiful young woman. He wiped his face with both hands and held them there, pressing his cheeks together in the "Oh my" expression, then laughed seriously, "from her first breath to adulthood went by so fast it was like being …

Passing Fields

On a train,
passing so many fields
like life hurrying by
pleasant green fields and
dying brownfields.
Then meadows, pastures,
and more fields.
Just like people,
Weary people,
joyful people,
desperate people,
content people,
angry people, and
uncertain people.
People
passing through life,
passing life by,
passing life forward,
like the quickly passing
fields

"My daughter! Your daughter! Our children are like fields! That has been my overall experience, he said quite frankly. Life, rushing forward, resembling a sprinter in a marathon and carrying all humanity with it. Even on the days that seem to drag on forever, time is steadily moving. Bringing us to our finish line, never taking a breather or a power pause to reenergize itself because life doesn't get tired; we do! We grow old! Our children will grow old! Their children will grow old on this journey that we are taking. But, life itself doesn't get tired! It just follows a path and continues moving forward. So, we make the best of it all, and hopefully we learn to appreciate our different fields."

He sighed then smiled and continued his reflections metaphorically...

Meadows and Mountains

Youth is like the splendor of spring.
Its various colored flowers
with soft petals fragrant and pretty,
and wild grass beneath bare feet.
It's the carefree heart of a child
walking through the meadows
towards the highlands.
Age is like winter's chill,
brisk with winds
and snowflakes falling without control
then landing their fragile frames
on lonesome mountain peaks.
Age watches while youth runs
towards the hill,
through the flowers that fade
and the grass that withers.
Carelessly rushing through the grass
beneath their feet,
youth often miss the symbolism displayed
underneath their toes;
for under their feet is a picture of destiny,
the pattern of all things undergoing a change
Touched by the footprints of time.

"Time touches us all," he repeated adamantly, "and If we seriously look at life with the right perspective, we must reach this conclusion. Life is a combination of things we can control and things we can't!

Nevertheless, we should keep in mind, that no matter how quickly life is moving and how uncontrollable it may be, life is a beautiful thing. So, as we climb our hills and run through our valleys, may we all consider the soil, the sky, the wind and what God is saying with them."

The Wise Man smiled and said reflectively, "I've noticed another fascinating thing in life besides the fact that it moves us like a sprinter in a marathon. There is always one thing that makes the difference in anything."

"For example, when I received my bank card in the mail; I opened the envelope and took it out. With it were the instructions concerning the card: how to activate it, the number to call to do so, etc. Well, as I glanced over the information quickly and by having my finger on the word, 'don't,' while holding the paper, it read, 'Write your pin number on the card or keep it with the card!' We all know that would have been a bad idea. But, just one word, makes a world of difference, and changes the outlook and outcome of everything, Consider the power of one" he stated and continued.

The Power of One

By one twist of fate, a full cup could be emptied.
By one turn of fate, an empty container could be filled.
There is just one step between this and that is simply
that the mystery of both sides of all things be revealed.
Between life and death, there is but one breath.
Between sorrow and joy, there is but one degree.
Just one significant venture could turn poverty into riches.
And by one extravagant gamble,
any wealthy person could become impoverished.
By one poor decision, freedom is halted.
By one judicial grant, freedom is returned.
In one moment, a crucial lesson could be missed.
In one moment, a vital lesson could be learned.
Due to one critical decision, there can be peace or war.
There is often one thin line between compassion and hate.
It takes just one bad-tempered person to tip the scales,
and a talk could be turned into a furious debate.
One blink of an eye separates light from the darkness.
One choice in this life gives man heaven or hell.
One slip of the tongue could make someone feel worthless.
One remark kindly spoken can make a person feel well.
Just one step will always make a difference.
Just one thing will always set the stage.
Just one word will change any sentence.
Just one number and it's another page.
Just one smile, and a heart could be gladdened.

Just one touch and hurt could be relieved.
One glimpse of truth, and a mind could be enlightened
as by one little lie, people are deceived.
One right turn or left, and a thing is loosened or tightened.
By one simple gesture, a mood may be lessened or heightened.
One moment in any life by the slightest turn of position
may make that one moment a life-changing revelation.
For in every solitary moment, it can be discovered,
that every single moment is unlike any other.
By one twist of fate, a full cup could be emptied.
By one turn of fate, an empty vessel could be filled.
There is just one step between this and that is simply
that the mystery of both sides of all things be revealed.

"Therefore, since life has its pattern and designs plus the power of one. The wisest thing we can do is roll with it, giving our greatest effort not to miss the small details while embracing all the uncontrollable shifting life presents." The Wise Man looked around the room and shared his next thoughts as playfully as a father encouraging his children.

Years

The spring
of life will pass;
winter comes quickly...
Tick tock, tick tock, tick tock,
youth flees steadily.
Soft meat, vegetables, soup,
eyes going dim.
Shoot! My back's out again!
It's not so easy remembering and
to forget things is not so hard.
Sometimes it's tough to walk.
For some, it's hard to talk.
And every day presents another card.
But wise aging lips
kiss the flower of sweet youth
tenderly goodbye.
Not to look back,
not to remorse
No tears to cry.

Therefore, my dear friends and acquaintances, and all others
gathered here …

My Parting Words

If
by chance
illness overcomes me
and you hear that it has me
laid up somewhere on a deathbed.
In that hour, no matter how it is said,
"He's gone, he passed away in his sleep, or he's dead."
This is the day that the years ushered in, the one that the
Creator's finger pointed to.
In that day,
Cut and send no flowers that they may die also.
Cut and send no flowers that they may adorn a casket
of bronze, brass, or gold plates or tones.
Let mine be a simple unfinished pine box.
Let no tears of sorrow wash your faces,
nor the weight of pain adorn your hearts.
Do not fill the room with gloom;
let tears of joy sprinkle the seeds of your lives
so that you all may continue to grow until each of you
reach that appointed time.

If
you choose
to speak, tell no lies,
paint no rosy pictures.
Tell the truth, be honest, and say what's in your heart.

Spit it out, get right with God.
I'll leave without any malice in my heart.
Laugh! Laugh! Yes, continue laughing! And
ff you cannot find it in your heart to laugh,
then at least smile.
Take a good look at the figure in that box
and think about the good things
that I may have said or done.

If
I said
or did something
to you back in the day
that caused you to be angry,
and you're still carrying it, stop now and look back
and realize that it did not affect or change me.
It only affected you.
I will be gone and like me, release the pain and anger.
Go free and never give anyone that much power over you again.
Laugh. Laugh. Laugh,
my friends! Eat, drink, and be merry!

"Wouldn't that be the best thing to do! Realizing there's no way of getting any moment back nor our loved ones when they pass away. Time will move us all away and time is the only true healer. Therefore, my attitude is to celebrate life every day with all the energy I have. And when a friend or loved one dies, I try to fully commemorate that life by continuing to live mine as joyously as possible while remembering all that their presence was to me. The memory of them is the treasure we keep. As I said, "Life will take you and me down its path, and there's no getting around it. So, be merry as you journey through life."

Part IV

Broadening the
Brush Strokes

The mood and atmosphere in the room were breathtakingly serene, like whispering wind ruffling flowers mysteriously in a meadow or waves quietly pushed to shore by an unseen hand.

He had very passionately shared his thoughts as he spoke of life, death, and time—those great realities and the destiny that lies before us all. We had breathed in his sentiments like oxygen and held our breath for as long as possible not to let those words escape. His eyes were closed, giving him a guru's appearance. He was at peace with everything around him. His lips parted slightly, sucking in the ambience of the room. He exhaled slowly as if to make sure that his breath was released entirely back into the atmosphere. His neatly trimmed beard and mustache seemed to speak before he did.

"I've concluded there are a few main ingredients to happiness in one's life. It is my presupposition; it may not be yours. Nevertheless, since I am sharing my experiences, I may as well share this—take time to smile! Follow love. Remember the bells. Gain through loss. Don't be lofty and high-minded. Love always loves, Oh, excuse me, were those restatements? Yes, they were! But, wouldn't you agree that smiling and loving and laughing, and remembering your bells should be the type of reiteration we cling to and tolerate? Because if life has taught me anything, it has indeed taught me this—it can throw a changeup or curveball at any given moment."

He continued semi-humorously with his next thoughts.

Really

One long-ago July evening
when what we thought
was the perfect day wasn't,
everything became clear.
Things are not always
what they seem to be.
That person you thought
was the one, wasn't.
What seemed like
the perfect job wasn't.
What you thought was good,
turned out bad.
What you considered the best became the worst.
You wanted an A+ and got an F-.
What appeared cool and bold
was sadly cowardice and foolishness.
What looked very scary
wasn't so horrifying after all.
What you thought you couldn't do,
you did!
Your organized plan failed,
 and your unorganized plan succeeded.
What seemed awkward and confusing
 turned out well and orderly.
Your friend deceived you,
 your enemy became your companion,

and what seemed endless, ended.
So,
what appeared to be this or that
was not what it was.
Or, was it?

"Yes, the vicissitudes of life have been great instructors, and I've learned to listen to their voice, giving my best effort to grow in each situation without being stiff or unyielding to the lesson presented. However, some folk do not learn until it's too late," He smiled and continued.

Mr. Woodspring

On Providence Drive, there was a house
with a lovely white picket fence,
Victorian windows, a massive lawn,
and one ole grumpy resident.
There's an oak tree towering in the yard,
the flowers were neatly in a row,
red roses were planted just for show,
facing towards Lakeshore Boulevard.
There were the sounds of kids and daily traffic.
There were the sounds of birds chirping in the air.
There were the sounds of a poor man's misery.
There were the sounds of that unhappy man's despair.
Mr. Woodspring didn't care much for birds,
but each morning they were the first thing that he heard.
They would penetrate his frustrated silence.
He'd retaliate in fits of rage and violence.
Mrs. Woodspring left the home some time ago,
and her secret reasons the neighbors think they know.
But, being cautious they never told him so,
but how could he not know?
Then, one day, as the spring birds sang,
one cheerful bird tapped on his windowpane.
Mr. Woodspring, in anger unrestrained,
grabbed his 45.
He shot at the fowl but struck glass and wood.
He missed the bird, but it still felt good,

He realized then, in no way should
he let them stay alive.
So, he grabbed a can of kerosene,
and in some strange way, he should have seen,
the reckless plan and his faulty scheme
would inevitably backfire.
But, in his anger and his fury,
in deep rage and in a hurry,
he struck the match and did not worry,
until he saw the fire.
On Providence Drive, there *was* a house
with a lovely white picket fence,
Victorian windows, a massive lawn,
and one very, very grumpy resident.

The mood in the room had shifted immensely and was popping with questions!

Was this just a metaphoric example the Wise Man had slipped in to make a point? Did the Wise Man merely use this hyperbolic language to grab our imaginations and get our full attention? If so, he had honestly done that. The explosive fireworks of humorous curiosity swirled around the room like smoke as we reflected on the tale of Mr. Woodspring.

"Listen! Listen!" he said, interrupting our thoughts. "Some folks can't let go of anger or distrust, and stubbornness has caused many people to crash and burn. Some people have become so influenced by their suspicion and disbelief that they feel like they can't trust anyone. They spend their lives being skeptics of almost everything and are too stubborn to give anything a chance. It becomes a phobia. There are people so engulfed with anger and doubt, it turns them into fools. It's sad but true," stated the Wise Man and shared another thought.

Two Fools

Twiddle Dee-Dee
rode next to Twiddle Dee Dum
one ate an apple; one ate a plum.
One rode a horse, one rode a donkey,
one with a pet cat, one with a pet monkey.
Both full of pride, both full of vanity,
one blinded by suspicion,
one stooped with insanity.
Both completely selfish
and eccentric, but then how be it;
they were both so egocentric
that neither of them could see it.
Twiddle Dee Dum said to Twiddle Dee-Dee
"I'll outwit you,
before you outsmart me."
Twiddle Dee-Dee said to Twiddle Dee Dum
"Boy, I'm smarter than you,
going, coming, and then some."
So, onward, they rode with no further words spoken
till simultaneously, side by side
they both started choking.
Now both thought the other was trying
to pull a con game but they were both sadly dying.
Then Dee fell from the horse and Dum off the donkey.
leaving behind the cat and monkey.
Leaving behind the sun and the rain,

leaving behind the joy and the pain,
it seems both sadly passed with a vain thought of glee,
"You will never in this life make a fool out of me."

The Wise Man gave a sad chuckle and shook his head at the end of his parable. "There will be curves that come in our lives but it's how we face those curves and handle them that makes a world of difference. Some people don't deal with curves well. They get angry, defensive, and often become distrusting. They become dishonest and often get discouraged.

The list goes on and on. Yet, some people cause curves in their own lives and the lives of others. Curves, boy those curves," said the Wise Man.

"You know what gets my goat," said an elderly man nearly shouting. "What gets your goat?" asked the Wise Man inquisitively. "Do share!"

The man continued in an agitated voice. "When people get to the point that they think they know it all, and no one can tell them anything, that irritates the crap outta me!"

"I know a few people like that," interjected a burly man and a middle-aged woman. The elderly man continued, "They believe they have it all together. People like that irritate me more than the angry ones or the distrusting folk." "Me too," chimed the burly fella and the middle-aged woman, sounding as agitated as the old man. "I think," he said stating his opinion, "People with anger issues may have some legitimate reason for being angry, as well as those who have trust issues, may have a sound cause for their distrust. I can even tolerate stubborn people at times; they may not know how to deal with their problems, or they may have a valid reason to be stubborn. Stubborn can mean determined or adamant which in my opinion is not always a bad thing." He made a face and continued, "But people who think they know it all, I've never understood their reasoning!"

"Maybe it's insecurity," replied the Wise Man, "but who knows for sure what makes the know-it-all tick. However, you brought up an excellent point concerning angry and suspicious people; they may have reasons beyond our understanding of their anger or frustration."

"That's right," interjected the burly fella, almost cutting the Wise Man off mid-sentence. "Some people do crazy things. Who knows why people act as they do! We have psychiatrists and psychologists trying to help people like that every day. Clinics and everything, and we still have people full of madness," he continued. "That guy, Mr. Woodspring, and those two other guys, whew! Not good!" Shaking his head, he repeated "Not good at all."

The Wise Man quickly interjected a thought. "There's an enormous tragedy in uncontrolled anger, foolish stubbornness, and unmerited suspicion."

"Yeah," responded the burly man, "I agree with you completely! Those guys were crazy beyond lunacy and very dangerous in my opinion." There was a subtle display of humor in the way he had expressed his last statement, yet it was apparent he was serious about what he said. "My theory," continued the big guy, "is stop the madness before it stops you!"

"That's an interesting thought," said the Wise Man, an interesting view indeed. And I certainly see sense in it. But, controlling anger and suspicion is not always as easy for the person under its influence to do as people sometimes believe."

The Wise Man took his eyes off the big man momentarily and shifted his gaze back to the crowd.

"You see, my friends," said the Wise Man glancing back at the man and woman who had just commented, then back to the crowd. "We may not know precisely why people act the way they do or their reasons for their behavior, yet some things are clear. Foolishness, stubbornness and uncontrolled anger, as well as being unduly suspicious are very unhealthy. When foolishness, stubbornness and uncontrolled anger hold a person captive, and unmerited suspicion holds a person prisoner, the chains are hard to break. Anger can blind a person and keep them in darkness while stubbornness can cover a person's eyes to all reality outside of their own. And, unnecessary suspicion keeps a person off balance at best and in the worst-case scenario can cause them to be accusatory to the degree of slander and quite cynical in their ways."

"Overly stubborn, angry, and suspicious people are trapped; they are worse than the living dead. However, don't misunderstand this truth. There is a moment in everyone's life where a degree of stubbornness is healthy, even necessary, as well as moments when anger is beneficial. And, there are indeed times when we should be cautious. Yet, anger that hurts others and causes harm, is not good. A suspicion that destroys innocent people is not healthy. And, stubbornness that destroys relationships is not beneficial. They're potholes!

And I wholeheartedly agree with both of you; a know-it-all is like a tree that doesn't give shade or a dam that doesn't hold back water. I believe with all my heart that the unduly stubborn, the uncontrolled angry, the overly suspicious people and the know-it-all need help and the healing touch of God. Let's pray for each other that we don't fall into these traps. Let's also pray for the deliverance of those that already have!"

The Wise Man smiled and asked a rhetorical question. "Have you ever considered how valuable relationships are to humans?" Everyone appeared to be reflecting on the inquiry.

The Wise Man continued his thoughts. "I often think about relationships and their importance in our lives. It's been discovered that relationships are so crucial to the human makeup that sometimes when an individual is without some form of relational interaction, the individual will make up imaginary people to communicate with, even if it's just their alter ego. It seems a bit crazy, but it's factual according to scientific research."

"So, friendships and relationships are quite vital to us as people. Sadly, we sometimes misuse our friendships, mishandle relationships, and destroy them and ourselves in the process. I know my examples of Mr. Woodspring and the two fools were somewhat extreme, but often we call ourselves friends and act more like enemies. We profess love and conduct ourselves in ways that resemble hate. We make covenants and break them. We promise to build each other up and then we tear each other down, especially when pride, anger, foolish stubbornness, and undue suspicion, creep in. These love and friendship killers strangle all parties involved."

He half-grinned and looked carefully around the room, letting his eyes go slowly from face to face.

"Would you agree? he slightly grinned again. "That anyone who professes to love another person should display the true character of love. Would you also agree, a friend should be someone you can depend on? I'm convinced real friends have a genuine concern for your well-being at heart. They're not at all like those two fools or Mr. Woodspring. A true friend is not in an egotistical competition with you, nor will they battle against you senselessly. And, even when their blatant honesty causes pain, that's not their motivation. Real friends will rejoice when you rejoice and hurt when you hurt. They'll go the extra mile with you. They're those people that gives you the shirt off their back even if they must go without one for a while. They are the best of people in life. Then," he added with emphasis, "make sure when you come across one you recognize them for who they are because a good friend is hard to find. Please don't let your preconceptions and stereotypical thoughts prevent you from gaining a lifelong companion. A lifelong friend!" he continued, as he made an important observational point.

The Road to Friendship

It is beyond my wildest imagination how we as beings
of the human race, can ever conceive of making friends
because the road to friendship is filled
with so many obstacles, that we must overcome.
There are so many eyes which admire us,
hearts that adore us,
hands that reach out to us and real friends that are waiting for us.
But the road is filled with the stones of criticism,
curves of self-righteousness, tunnels of insecurity,
and potholes of prejudice and stubbornness.
Plus, the one-way streets of preconception
and the shadows of doubt.
We have all passed up a lot of friends solely because we
judged them by their color, creed or national origin.
Often, we stand on the corners of the one-way streets
with preconceived ideas and pelt possible friends with the
stones of criticism, then run into the tunnels of insecurity and
hide in the shadows of doubt.
We go foolhardily around the curves of self-righteousness
and get stuck in the potholes of prejudice and stubbornness.
We do not look for the qualities that they might have, but we
judge them by the way they look.
Some, we marvel over, because of their glamour, yet others
we ignore because we perceive them as being ugly.
We often embrace the exciting ones and automatically call
them friend while they empty our pockets and vanish in

the wind. When, if ever! will we accept the person for their inherent qualities?

The crowd remained quiet. Not an uneasy quiet, more a quiet like when something is supposed to happen, but you're not sure what.

"Think of this," the Wise man said, a bit troubled, "what if the tables were turned? What if we were the friend that was overlooked through discrimination? What if you and I were the people that got passed up without a second glance? What if you, with all your qualities, were never seen as a person of value to be befriended? Or, if the friend you believed you knew very well cut you off for reasons that you have never been privy to? How would you feel if people only call you friend because they want to use you? They value your resources but not you." The Wise Man paused and continued, "How would you receive that? How would you deal with it? You see, life is about placing yourself in another's shoes and taking a walk not only with those shoes but also metaphorically with those feet. May I give you another piece of wood to burn as fuel for thought? Imagine this …if someone had to say to you …

Who Am I?

Who am I?
I know who I am.
I'm that person that you never think of until you see me.
I'm the one who never receives a return phone call from you.
You remember me when our paths cross by chance.
You greet me gracefully with a smile, and say, "Hey, man! How are you doing?"
"Let's do lunch, give me your telephone number,"
and with a smile, I give it to you again, and I say,
"I've called you, and you did not return my calls,"
(and I'm thinking, I'll starve before this lunch comes about).
Apologetically, you reply, "Sorry about that, I've been
Busy, busy, busy!"
Now, I am a thinking man, and, in my mind, I've been assorting tangled thoughts that said to me, "You're not important,"
and with that, I concluded
with importance, there is the burden of responsibility.
Importance will never burden me because
I'm an irresponsible personality.
In my conclusion, busy, busy, busy means I am not high on your list of priorities.

Who am I?
I am the same person that you praise when our paths cross and you are in the presence of others.

The response is always the same,
"Hey, man! How are you?" I am introduced as your friend, and with the hissing of an exhale, you say,
"Whew! This brother is heavy!
You should talk to him.
This brother is out there, let's get together soon.
This brother has some stuff for your mind."
Now I'm thinking, Man,
and in my mind, I have been assorting tangled thoughts that questions that introduction.
Why did he say I was heavy? Did he say that I was overweight?
Why did he say I was out there? I was standing next to him.
Did he just say that I was selling some type of controlled substance?
Why does he need to talk to me?
Fate never let us interact by accident, so that introduction must have been a compliment.

I know who I am.
I know that I'm your friend, yet your actions do not indicate that you are mine.

"Has anyone here ever experienced that?" he asked solemnly with a concerned expression pasted on his face. "Have you ever experienced the reality of someone calling you their friend and their actions display a different picture?" Several guests' facial expressions were indicating yes although the Wise Man didn't get any verbal responses.
"It's an awkward place to be," he stated sadly, then somberly he continued, "It's also sobering!"

"Maybe you haven't experienced verbal friendship that lacks sincerity," he said as his eyes closed briefly and opened again. "Maybe your uphill experience was not being able to reconcile your friendship when it was damaged. You knew in your heart you were a true friend, and you also recognized their continual indifference. Yet, in spite of that you still continued reaching out. Something in you wanted that broken relationship repaired and that pushed you to give all you could."

"Don't beat yourself up for giving your all." said the Wise Man seriously. There wasn't more you could give! Sometimes things just don't work out like you plan them." He rubbed his shirtsleeve as if to brush off a piece of lint and said, "Let me share this tale as an example."

Two mice ran through the grass together. They sang a song of celebration as they journeyed through the field. They had been friends for several years and had enjoyed many adventures together. These two mice had faced so many adversities together that it seemed nothing could shake their friendship. No argument, no disagreement, no misunderstanding had ever caused a wedge in their companionship; they seemed inseparable.

One day, as they were running through the fields, it began to rain. It rained harder than it had ever rained before. It was the beginning of a hurricane. In the middle of that field was a dilapidated building. A few feral cats lived in the building or, so it was said; no one knew for sure if that was fact or fiction. However, the winds and the rain were facts and the conditions were getting worse, quickly. These two mice were faced with a decision and as they discussed the situation and weighed out their options, they could not agree on what was best to do. They became frustrated with each other and began to argue and as the argument progressed, their disagreement led to a terrible dispute. A dispute which became so intense that it caused them to go their separate ways. So, on that dark rainy day facing an old beat up building and possible feral cats, two good friends allowed themselves to be pushed apart.

The Wise Man looked around to make sure he had everyone's attention. Then, he said with deep emotion, "it wasn't the storm, or the different ideas, or the thought of the cats, that caused their problem. It was their unwillingness to work through it together that produced the split."

The Wise Man scanned the audience again taking notice of their expressions. Many were still in reflection, and a few looked dazed and frustrated. In the front section, midway back from the platform, a few people were tossing strange looks back and forth like a ball in a game of tennis. A bit left from the tennis match,

a slender, fashionably dressed lady in her late 30s stared at a female who appeared to be the same age. The staring woman locked her gaze on the other like a lion on a hunt. She never allowed her stare to drop or move away from the other woman's face. The only thing that concealed it partially was the wide-brimmed hat she wore. The other lady in this semi-staring contest was delicate and petite; she held her gaze as long as she could, and her fiery red cheeks gave away clues that suggested these two women were dealing with some type of misunderstanding or problem between them.

The Wise Man noticed the situation and cleared his throat to make sure the audience was focused completely on him.

"A friendship can be rescued," he said with deep sentiment.

It doesn't matter how long it's been since the friends last spoke to each other, or how angry they may be with each other. The thing that keeps friendships from being repaired or from moving forward is when the friends are too stubborn to find a middle ground or have decided to move on. Therefore, friends must be honest, open-minded people willing to share with each other and willing to give and take. Selfishness and unforgiveness gives friendships flat tires.Since history plays an important part in every friendship, if you're trying to restore or repair your friendship use the positives that build good relationships, don't rehash the negatives that ruin them."

"If you have a dispute, no matter how hefty the disagreement, don't allow that to destroy your companionship. Always seek to save the relationship if possible, even if it has been severely damaged. In the event you cannot be friends any longer, at least be cordial; being an enemy to someone formerly considered a friend can be heavy because resentment and anger are heavy rocks to carry. As I said, if the day comes when there is no repairing the friendship, bid them farewell without regret or bitterness. That's the wise thing to do; anything else can cause more trouble than its worth."

The Wise Man paused and allowed his eyes to peruse their faces again, waiting for anyone that may have wanted to express a thought, and then said …

"There is something very dear to me that I would like to read to you." He pulled out the piece of paper he had placed in his pocket earlier, put on his reading glasses and began reading it endearingly.

A Letter to My Friend

It takes courage to confide in anyone.
So, each time you trust me with
your most intimate thoughts and concerns,
it's humbling.
I appreciate your confidence in me
that you consider me to have
enough sound judgment and common sense
to assist you in working out problems
and in finding the best course of action
to follow during challenging junctures of your life.
Thanks for allowing me to be candid
and for seeing me as a person of integrity.
Thanks for allowing yourself the liberty
to lean on me and for lending me
the opportunities to be a shoulder of support to you.
Thank you for allowing me to help
you carry your burdens
and thanks for assisting with mine.
Be encouraged,
good things come to the enduring heart
to those that do not faint,
to those that hold on and don't give up.
I wish you only success,
and may you find the strength and courage
to push forward,
especially in the face of adversity.

Consider your hurdles challenges
to strengthen you for bigger things.
And look at your valleys as steps
to take you to mountain tops.
May your darkest night display the presence of hope,
no matter how small the light may be.
And I pray you'll continue to be a candle for others
as God's light reflects through you.
May you always find love, peace, and joy
present and thriving in your heart.
And may you never lose focus of the bigger picture
by losing focus of who God says you are
and where your destiny's taking you.

To my friend and companion,
Your true friend

"My buddy wrote that letter to me not too long ago. Well, shortly before he passed, and it's still hard knowing he's gone but each day gets better. Believe me, we had our many disagreements, but I realized he wasn't perfect, nor am I. He was a great dude! A true friend!" The Wise Man cleared his throat again and refolded the paper, placing it back in his pocket as carefully as he had taken it out. He had a concerned look on his face; the pensive look on a face that causes squinting of the eyes as if he was trying to focus on something in the distance that he was having a hard time seeing.

It was apparent he was in a struggle. He was desperately trying to gather his thoughts while attempting to maintain his focus. Blinking rapidly, he let out a thick breath of air. Then, he rubbed the left side of his head with his left hand and held it there momentarily, repeating a few times. Appearing as if he was trying to erase invisible lines from his forehead or help stimulate his thoughts and what had seemed an eternity had only taken a few seconds, he said, "I have had my share of acquaintances over the years, and I have fantastic friends now."

He wiped his forehead again, looking up in reflection and continued onward. "Reading that note from my buddy caused me to think of my childhood. I grew up in the times of segregation. It wasn't so common for black and white children to be together as they are now. Things are different nowadays and thank goodness for change, but I can vividly remember one of my dearest childhood friends."

My Friend

My friend had eyes like emeralds, hair like corn silk. We'd often visit each other and share some cookies and milk.
Each day my friend would knock on the door and say, "Can you come out and play today?"
Mom would stand at the door and watch us
as we dashed away to the nearby meadows where we would often play.
The days weeks and months slipped into years and somehow the years manifested tears.
For upon one dark and painful day, my friend was taken away.
Not a year has passed or for that fact, a day has passed that I haven't missed that sweet little voice which would say,
"May he come out to play?"
Parents are cruel was the thought I carried in my mind
because they took my friend and left me behind.
Again, the years have slipped away while I sat by the door with the hope that I would hear a knock and my friend would say, would you like to come out to play?"
I still recall the meadows along the rolling hills where we'd pick wildflowers, roses, and daffodils.
We would race with our prizes across the meadows
and down the rolling hills to our homes where we'd present to our mothers the limp and crushed little bouquets of roses and daffodils. Now that I'm a parent, a thought knocked upon the door of my mind, and a voice did say,
"Father, what games will these two grow up and play?"

And with that thought, they up and moved away.

Somehow life repeats itself; children come to my door and say, "Can my friend come out to play?"

The Wise Man paused again and rubbed his forehead once more. "Yes," he said sighing as he reflected, "I had a friend in those dark, cruel days that was as white as snow with a heart as pure as gold. We had so much fun being us that it was growing into love.

Her family did not approve of us being so close, and my family was terrified for me. It was downright painful because we were terrific friends that had forgotten the world of colors. My friend was torn between her feelings for me and her family's disapproval while I was battling her family's criticism and my family's fear. So, that crazy day arrived that I sensed would inevitably come, the day that I had been expecting, the day that she would announce she had to stop seeing me entirely. I can clearly remember the words I shared with her …

Sometimes at Night, I Fight

Sometimes at night, I fight the sleep that lingers
in the darkness waiting for me to become quiet
that it can pull the wool over my eyes and make me dream
lovely dreams that are laced with trickery and outright lies.
Sometimes at night, I fight the light that sneaks into the night
and summons fatigue to come and wrestle with me until my
body is utterly devoid of resistance.
Then sleep throws sand in my eyes
to render them blind to everything but rest.
I fight sleep and fatigue because I believe if I give in,
they will steal my thoughts of you away.
Sometimes at night, I fight the reality
that all those sleepless and restless nights that I spent holding
you and kissing you in my thoughts are as empty as those
tricky lying dreams.
Sometimes at night, I fight the thought of thinking
of you and having you with me in my dreams,
but it is better than not having you at all.
And then again, I do not have you at all.
Sometimes at night, I fight back the tears
that flood my eyes like twin waterfalls,
churning and tossing the emotions
that beat against my heart
like debris that is being washed to distant fields and streams.
Sometimes at night, I fight back the thoughts
that I should stop thinking of you.

At night, I fight.

He shifted in the seat a few times like a child with a nervous condition, then settled himself again and continued to elaborate on that painful time.

Thoughts

Thoughts, who are they, and why do they always bring me you without you?
Thoughts bring memories—sometimes kind, sometimes mean-spirited.
Some are filled with joy, others with pain.
Some are loosely clothed in sunshine; others are tightly fitted in the rain.
I am like the wheel of infinity, endlessly spinning around, never recognizing the beginning and fearful that I will realize the end.
Thoughts ushered in reality sprinkled with stardust,
illuminated in moon glow fashioned by time
and attracted and matured by sunlight.
My thoughts brought music without musicians
yet performed by musicians,
then thought brought me rhythm that allowed me to dance.
Again, never dancing with rhythm.
Thoughts are the endless spinning wheel of infinity that will bring you or carry me to the beginning that always was
an ending that still will be, "fate."

"That's precisely what I told her as she stood there doing all she could to conceal the pain that was aching in her heart. It wasn't her fault that we could not be together, and I didn't want to blame our parents. Society was all around us and weighing in on us heavily with its unyielding brutality against interracial relationships and its general hatred for blacks. Hatred is always horrible! Oh, man! If anyone else had discovered our secret I probably wouldn't be here sharing my life's story with you today, nah, not at all! Things were very different at that time, very, very different! America is still a far cry from where it should be, but it's better in many ways than it was."

No one moved a muscle it seemed as he shared his thoughts about the hurt, he had from losing a friend to hatred until one youth raised his hand like a student trying to get the attention of the teacher.

"Sir!" said the slender teenager with the neon orange t-shirt, faded jeans, and ultra-white teeth in braces. "Which was the most difficult for you— losing your best friend or your girlfriend? I mean, even though she didn't die, she kinda died in a different way." He was looking at the Wise Man with youthful curiosity.

The young man was seeking answers; his urgency was evident in his stance. Arms crossed, head slightly leaning to one side, never once shifting his gaze waiting for the Wise Man's response. "I mean, do you see what I'm saying," he repeated once more with sudden hand gestures.

"Yes, I do feel what you're saying," responded the Wise Man with youthful colloquialism. "And yes, I certainly do understand your questions and to give you a sincere answer—both hurt but in different ways. And what you said is correct in a sense, 'they both did depart,' and I didn't get either of them back. However, I must say my buddy's death came as more of a surprise to me than her saying goodbye did, so I suppose in a way, I was more prepared for her leaving then I was for his. Maybe it was because her family's choice took her away from me, and time did not. Time, not his choice, took him. I hope that answers your questions." He nodded his approval, and the Wise Man refocused his attention on continuing his narrative.

"Before I move forward, let me quickly share a thought that always helps me stay focused and encouraged. Bear in mind that life is about breath, that fields are passing quickly, that the power of one is significant, plus, we often gain through loss. I use these concepts as compasses, and they have helped me enormously.

However, I rely on the strength of God to make me fruitful. So, I have learned to say there will always be …

A Better Day!

Don't worry about me,
I'll be alright
I've crossed this bridge before
by day and by night.
The darkness tried to scare me, and
put me in a horrible fright
but it was the joy of the Lord within me
that gave me the strength to fight.
It was a perfect peace that held me,
and its fire that did convey
a certainty in my soul saying,
"No matter come what come may
I will make it through these hardships,
I will see a brighter day,
I will land on peaceful shores,
I will sail in quiet waters.
Tranquility shall be my companion once more
in my labors and my quarters.
True faith always brings order
where chaos tries to abound.
And where misfortune tried to triumph,
God's love kept me sound.
Troubles are destined to meet me
but if I never meet them with defeat,
I can face them with the same expectations
of victory, every time we meet.

For if I can face tragedy today with joy,
I'll laugh hilariously tomorrow.
Not just because I overcame
but because joy defeated sorrow.

"That's how I was successful young man, that's how I made it through—I trusted the Lord! I focused on a better day and left the negatives in the past. That doesn't mean that memories and thoughts don't arise, they do! However, I focus on the good times and move on because that's what we have in the end, memories, only memories. And, it's your decision as to which ones you want to hold onto. Yes, indeed young man, people move on like time, as time never stops! Think about this" the Wise Man suggested thoughtfully

That's Life

Life goes on
regardless of how we feel.
All our joys or grievances
cannot stop the wheel
of time from turning steadily
towards another second.
Not concerned with our emotions
from pure hate to total affection.
Tragedies and triumphs
are like baggage we carry through life;
rewards of our achievements
and the pains of each sacrifice.

So, if nothing else is definite, nothing guaranteed, when it relates to people remaining in or exiting from our lives—the one thing that life guarantees is ...

Moving Forward

Time keeps rolling like a wheel
indifferent, however never standing still and
endlessly moving forward towards its destiny.
Cleverly binding present, future, and history,
time marches on unseen and soundless,
steady as an army without boundaries.
Never looking back from whence it came
to time past, present, and future are the same.
Time has no disgust or appreciation
for the rise or the fall of men and nations
but casually observes without a notion
of the ever-changing course of forward motion.
Time has neither an enemy nor a friend
and calls all to the same predestined end.
It alone feels no misery, shame, or dismay
but steadily moves towards another day
guided by the hand of God divine and
never losing pace or wasting time.

"Since time will continue moving forward and I must run with it, I figured I might as well carry joy because it is so much better, and it is so much lighter than all of that other stuff we carry around with us. Like thoughts of regret or holding grudges and unforgiveness in our hearts or worrying continuously about things we have no control over—that's a heavy burden and an enormous waste of time. Thoughts of joy and peace; that's my energy booster!"

There it was again, that warm magnetic smile like sunshine landing on Lake Tahoe or moonlight dancing on the shores of Chesapeake Bay. His eyes slowly scanned the faces in the room, but he didn't focus his attention on anyone specifically. When he spoke again his voice had changed slightly. "Please close your eyes and concentrate on my words." He laughed and said, "Don't worry, I'm not trying to hypnotize anyone; I only want to challenge you with a few questions. Furthermore, I'm not looking for you to share your answers with me, those are yours … take them with you. Are you ready for the questions?" He smiled warmly and then continued to speak in a reassuring voice expressing his inquisitions.

Where Did Your Thoughts Go?

Hello, Heart,
Where did your thoughts go last night?
Did they walk hand in hand?
On the sand of the beach in Waikiki,
or did they fly on the wings of love
to the shores of faraway places?
Did they feel joy when they met people with lovely and smiling faces?

Hello, Love,
Where did your thoughts go last night?
Did they hide in the shadows of a dream unrealized?
or did they touch the heart of love unfulfilled?
Where did your thoughts go last night?
Did they embrace memories
of the sad and lovely moments that left you alone to cry?
then kiss those memories goodbye.
Did they hold the dreams that never wore a frown?
Did they bring them home
and ask them to stick' around?

Hello, Dreamer,
Where did your thoughts go last night?
Did they ride on the wings of yesterday's fulfillment
or did they rest in the lap of yesterday's disappointments?
Did they embrace the joy of life

and a world of divine tranquility
or did they get into a fight with war and poverty?

Hello. Thinker,
Where did your thoughts go last night?
Did they knock upon the doors of your heart?
to ask if it would beat a path
at least to the edges of lost love's shadow to see
if they could touch that hand, to see that smile,
to hear that voice or to look into those eyes?
Hello thoughts, where did you go last night?

"I think you get my point; our thoughts take us many places and in many different directions. You may open your eyes," the Wise Man said and continued sharing his observations. "We can allow our thoughts to control us, or we can take control of our thoughts. As the German Theologian Martin Luther said, "Just because a bird flies over your head doesn't mean you must allow it to build a nest" (n.d.). We are challenged by thoughts all the time. Good ones and those that may not be so virtuous, positive or beneficial, but the power is within each person to change their way of thinking. That's one of the very reasons I didn't allow my thoughts to hold me captive when my friends were taken out of my life. That's how Luana feels about her cancer, and I share the same views. I had to let go of every thought that would hold me captive negatively because I realized no one else's thoughts could trap me as tightly as my own."

"Let's be humorously serious for a moment if there is such an animal. Some, of you are hearing me speak, but are thinking of at least two other things while you're listening to me. We can call it multi-tasking, or we can call it being scatterbrained. We can call it a lack of focus or we can call it semi-interested. We may call it being sidetracked by our other interests striving to get our total attention. And sometimes it's just the fleeting thoughts that blow through our minds like dust, settling and being wiped away as quickly as they came, that cause momentary distractions. There are many things we can call our minds when they go through those many channels of thought. It's just a matter of perspective in what we choose to call those moments, and those moments unquestionably come."

"The question is, what types of views are they and what kind of control do they have on your actions? Because we all have an opinion of ourselves and others."

"That's true," said a distinguished-looking, gray-haired gentleman. "That's what makes us who we are, our views. Well, let me rephrase that," the elderly gentleman said correcting himself. "We display who we are and how we think by our opinions of ourselves and by our views of others. And sometimes our views of others and ourselves can be inaccurate. An inaccurate view can lead to misjudgments and bias. And bias can lead to an avalanche of other misconceptions. At least that's been my experience and assessment. How do you see it?" he asked the Wise Man. The Wise Man responded …

If

If I carry my heart in my hand and my attitude on my sleeve, what would you think of me? If always and under all conditions, I wore a smile upon my face, would you see me as cold and uncaring, filled with joy, a phony, happy and carefree, or devoid of any other human emotion? If tears washed my face as constantly as the wind blows and as often as the sun rises and sets or the skin upon my face was dry cracked and wrinkled as old worn leather, and my clothing was dirty, smelly and torn, would you feel sorrow? Would you stop and reach out to me and offer me a gesture of sympathy, a moment of comfort or would you feel disdain and see me as a hopeless old fool? If you heard me scream out in agony because my body was broken and racked with pain, what would you do? If in my screaming I prayed for mercy and forgiveness for any evil thoughts, deeds, or feelings that I may have entertained or put into action, would you think that I was a weak and spineless sissy? Would you plug your ears mentally and go about your business without a second thought? If so, can you imagine that I may see you as cold, uncaring and filled with vanity? For all you saw in me was the human physical condition. Could you fathom that I may see you as devoid of any spiritual presence? For, you were seeing you but believing in your heart that you were seeing me!

"So, I wholeheartedly agree with you, sir. A person's perspective does at time not only reveal their view but may occasionally expose their character as well. And the saddest reality is that often their negative perspective of others is an unfortunate indicator of how spiritually void they are."

"Keep your mind filled with positive energy, so there is no room for negativity to enter. Helpful thoughts come from a positive mind and heart. The healthiest thoughts come from a relationship with God. He helps us see correctly," said the Wiseman smiling.

"That's very true," interjected the elderly gentleman. "I discovered through observation and learned from personal error in my walk with God the necessity of being careful of self-made opinions lacking truth or facts. It reveals the bias, prejudice, selfishness, self-righteousness, and ignorance in us."

"Yes, sir!" said the Wise Man. "I agree with you 100%. Because that has been my experience also. One's lopsided perspective can be as disorienting as drugs and just as debilitating. Thank you for your comments and your insight. It's always refreshing to hear the wisdom of others. I welcome such responses as yours; they are encouraging, and challenging."

"Does anyone else have something they would like to add or share? Please feel free to do so, maybe your comment will be just what the doctor ordered!"

"Sir, I have something I would like to say!" said a large woman from the crowd.

"Please share it with us," responded the Wise Man.

The woman began to speak. Her soft, soprano voice betrayed her size. "I have, for many years, watched people look at me with judgment and criticism in their eyes. I've also heard their slanderous remarks. I've listened to so many, 'fat girl' jokes, I could receive a Guinness book record."

"Nevertheless, what I want to say is, people can be so cruel, so heartless and uncaring when they have a misconstrued concept of themselves and an unclear view of others. Often people who don't know my character, my personality, or my medical condition, make nasty, snide remarks about my size and deformities, and those things are hurtful."

She was sobbing as she spoke, her voice was as soft as a gentle summer rain between sobs, but her words had the passion and force of a hurricane. "I'm not blaming anyone here, but I just had to let it out. I'm so sorry if I made anyone uncomfortable or made any of you feel like I was trying to make you feel guilty." She continued to sob. "That's not my intention at all!" She glanced at the Wise Man with tears in her eyes. "It's just, it's just…" she said trying to regain composure. "What you shared triggered something inside of me and I couldn't hold it in any longer."

The young man with the neon orange shirt and braces handed her a tissue. "I empathize with you," said the Wise Man. Some ladies in the group gathered around her and did what they could to console her. "I genuinely sympathize with you for I, too, have taken my share of insults over the years. And then he said quite empathetically …

Hello, Happiness

I have visited the home where the lonely live;
I did not like it. It's too dark and cold there.
I've looked through the eyes that were washed
with the tears of sadness,
where bleakness adorns them, and
I did not like it. It's too cold and wet there.
I've heard the voice that trembles when trying to speak words
when once uttered will have less value than used toilet paper.
I did not like the instability there.
I've felt the pounding of the heart that almost drowned out
the sound of that shaking voice that is trying desperately to
speak words that will bring joy back into your life. I did not
like it there either for I was disturbed by the noise and it was
too depressing there.
I've grasped at hands
that pulled away or laid limp and cold
and made my hands feel dirty and totally rejected.
I did not like it there either,
for there was no unity there.
Hello, happiness! I shall return home to you!

"I shall return home to happiness and joy in my heart and
not let anyone have the power to make me feel insignificant
or inferior again, or any less than valuable again. I will not
accept their view of my value! That was the decision I made
long ago, and I've held onto it with all my energy from that

day forward. I pray you will find the strength in yourself, with all the ebullience you can muster, to confidently say, 'I'm not what they think of me. I'm better than their views of me. None of them are superior to me, nor am I inferior to them. We are equals in the eyes of God, whether they accept it or not.' My perspective of myself changed when I decided to embrace me and love me as God loves me, with all my flaws and shortcomings. I am certain you will find peace and be strengthened when you do the same as I did."

Now, was it an easy journey to attain this mindset? Not at all, there were tears shed and anger released. There were cruel words that I said to myself and plenty of moments when I didn't feel like living. There were days when my self-esteem hit rock bottom and days when my apathetic attitude reached an all-time high. I had days when I was completely miserable, days when I wallowed in self-pity and days when I was overwhelmed with frustration. But, one day, yes, one very impactful day after listening to the wise, but simple words of a sermon preached in an old country church, I decided it was time to live for the Lord and me. I did not have to reach the status society set for me,

or accept the labels people had given me.

I only had to grab for what God already planned for my life. Yes, that was the day I decided to stop letting people declare to me who I am. That was the day I shouted in a different way. That was the day I said …

A Different Way

Good morning, World
Hello, New Day
You're the beginning
of a different way
in which I shall approach
the world
in which I live.
You're the dawn
of my attaining
that great pinnacle set before me.
Though at times it seems
the farthest star to reach,
you're the dawn of me believing
that I am a champion.
and that gave me such
an exuberant feeling
that goosebumps began forming
all over my anatomy.

"You are a unique person," said the Wise Man with a sigh. "Don't ever forget that the hands of God made you precious. See yourself that way and remember this," continued the Wise Man thoughtfully.

You are a Woman

You are a woman,
you are beautiful,
you were created that way
in spite of every scar
that life has given you,
in spite of every hurt
that you have ever felt,
or every mistake you have ever made.
You remain by design
a precious and unique flower
growing in the garden of humanity.
You are a treasure
that wise men adore
and fools mishandle.
You are a costly gem of gems,
jewel of jewels and
extraordinarily amazing.
And although you are often
misunderstood
mistreated, cheated, abused,
abandoned, and disgraced,
nothing can ever erase
the magnificent beauty that lives
deep inside of you,
destined to overflow
the moment you see yourself

as the precious woman
that you are.
A flower created by God
and very important to Him.

The Wise Man smiled at her with fatherly empathy and said, "Never forget that… never ever!"

Part V

Shades, Shadows and Pastels

The wise man stood up from the stool, giving him an opportunity to stretch his legs and walked down two steps which were temporarily placed there for the event. Clearing his throat and taking the last sip of water from its container, he then raised his hand and waved it slightly, saying, "I'm going to take a short break so I can gather my thoughts and decide which direction to go upon returning. I am truly honored by you all being here. Thank you for your patience!"

Beckoning one of the young men that had helped bring in the chair, he asked, "would you please bring me another bottle of water?" "Certainly," he replied. "We have other beverages available if you would like something else." "No, thank you," replied the Wise Man, "Water will do just fine. And would you take this with you and throw it in the trash can."

Nodding his head slowly signifying yes, he took the empty bottle, smiled and walked away. "Thanks again," said the Wise Man as he watched him go.

"Good kid!" said the burly fella standing a few feet from the Wise Man. "Yeah, I got that same impression," the Wise Man replied. "Do you know him?" "Yep, I do," said the fella, "I've known him for quite a while! His dad served in the Army; he didn't come home." "Sorry to hear that," the Wise Man replied. "Yes, it was very hard on him, but he's much better now. I guess that's just a part of life," said the big guy. "Just like you said earlier about your buddy, the good ones seem to go too fast, and we're stuck with the jerks—the idiots if you know what I mean!" "Well, not all of them are jerks, and I wouldn't call them idiots either," interjected the Wise Man, "but I understand your point."

The big fella folded his arms across his chest, made a noise in his throat which sounded like a frog gagging, and said,

"I was thinking about some of the things you've shared." "For example?" asked the Wise Man. The man replied, "The part when you spoke of fathers that are present yet missing." "Hmmm," slipped from the Wise Man's mouth before he could respond with a question or a statement. The burly fella continued talking. "I know a man like that, he was a hard worker, a very good provider, and his children didn't miss out on much of the material things, however, he never really spent a lot of quality time with them. You know what I mean?"

The Wise Man wasn't sure if he was speaking of himself or of someone he knew. "I understand that entirely," said the Wise Man, "My dad was also like that. Very dedicated to the job, the church, and some other things, but not into putting in that quality time with me. It's a recipe for strained relationships at times," said the Wise Man. "Amen!" replied the burly fella. "If you don't mind me sharing," stated the Wise Man, "I've always had a good work ethic; I got that from my dad, however, I noticed a pattern developing in me of being a workaholic, just like him. So, I decided to do all I could to keep a healthy balance. It's not easy, but it's possible and worth the extra effort and sacrifice." "That's true," said the man. "That's my opinion also. Not easy but definitely worth the extra effort!"

"Do you have any children?" asked the Wise Man. "Yes, I do," he replied. "Two boys and two girls." "I guess you can't beat that," replied the Wise Man.

They both chuckled at that remark. "Life can be extraordinary, but it can also be cruel," said the man as he looked up in reflection. "I have four great kids and I'll do anything for them, but my dad was very similar to yours in many ways!"

"Is he still around?" asked the Wise Man. "Yeah, but we don't talk much," he said, shrugging his big shoulders. "It's kind of off and on, here and there, once in a blue moon!" His eyes were now looking at the ground.

The Wise Man nodded his understanding and looked at the big guy with a smile that said, "I know that feeling!" The man continued, "But that kid right there, he's had it very rough. I guess life has a way of reminding us, when you think you've got it lousy, look around; there's someone in deeper mud!" "That's very true! Very, very true," said the Wise Man thoughtfully.

"Well, I guess you're about to continue," said the man. "Yeah, I am," responded the Wise Man. "I have a few more things to say, but it was good chatting with you, sir." "It was good talking with you also," replied the man as he moved away from the place where he had been standing.

The Wise Man returned to the platform, picked up the bottle of water that had been placed by his chair, raised it up in a gesture of thanks to the young man that had placed it there, untwisted the cap and took a long drink. He wiped his mouth with his hand and said, "I admit, one of the hardest things to do is to be honest, fair, and kind while sharing one's viewpoint, especially when it's a delicate subject being expressed or discussed. I understand that people don't generally like talking about the real issues they face unless it's in a private setting or with someone who shares their views."

"Nevertheless, there are some things that I will be sharing from this point onward that may ruffle a few feathers, may even cause downright anger to some of you because facing the truth is very difficult, especially when that truth exposes us to realities or uncovers lies we have embraced, told, or believed for years. And those uncomfortable issues which demand us to look at things that we don't want to see, or to see things that we would rather not face, are the very issues we need to discuss. I sincerely believe the only way to deal with difficult subjects is head on and with honesty. I've discovered that truth forces our hands in ways nothing else can, and when we accept it, the truth makes us free, but people will still try to find ways to get around it and deny its validity."

He rubbed his facial hair gently and continued. "Life can be extremely hard at times. It has so many ups and downs, and crazy sidetracks and setbacks, that test humanity. However, we must never lose hope; we must keep looking for the good in situations because better is always possible in any adverse condition. Good prevails when humanity makes the right choices." He paused for a second and spoke his next words in a more deliberate tone.

The Standoff

They stood
opposing each other
thinking yielding
would be a sign of weakness
and to unify
would steal their individuality.
However,
true strength is the ability
to expose and make vulnerable
to others that which
is truly one's self
without ever feeling
something is forfeited
in the exchange.

"That's the core conflict of America," said the Wise Man. "At its roots as a society there has never been a genuine acceptance of all people in this nation, in fairness and equality. There has never been, in the history of the United States, the equal give and take for all races and people that the constitution so adamantly declares and swears to defend."

"Many Americans still do not want to face the reality of imbalance in America because it's easier than looking the monster in the face. However, we must go forward looking truth in the eyes because the future of America depends on it."

The Wise Man began his new path with this preliminary thought as a gateway into the presentation of what he knew would be hard to swallow but necessary to eat; his words proceeded straightforwardly and were frank.

Falsely We Believe

Falsely we believe
that America is this great land of integrity,
that capitalism is not ruling democracy,
that our legal system is a system of equality,
and that the information machine is giving us information
without bias or hypocrisy.
It's believed that blacks,
which make up 13% of the American population,
are committing over 80% of the crimes.
That all police are concerned with real justice,
that judges are not biased and partial,
that Mexicans are "stealing jobs" from Americans,
and that in America, there is liberty and justice for all.
We falsely believe
that the tragedies and atrocities
we see and hear of are the losses and sorrows of others,
however, we are all in that family.
Anguish, sorrow, and doom await all in the adjoining room.
Oh yes, tragedies, atrocities, losses, and sorrow,
directly, or indirectly affects us all
while one family dines well, they often incorrectly believe
another family spends too much time wishing for better
while starving in the kitchen.
It's usually in fallacy imagined that the family in the big
house on the hill is playing a friendly game on the tennis

court, while an aggressive and contentious game of basketball is in session in the hood.

Falsely we believe we are safe in our homes
because we have burglar alarms, electronic listening, and observation devices because we have handguns, long guns, and police officers and soldiers with guns.
We hire police officers to serve and protect, but they have become militarized.
Often, they see the citizens that they are supposed to serve and protect as the enemy, especially when they are black and less so when they are white.
Many cops are casually shooting black citizens in the streets and swearing that they felt their life was being threatened.
What type of service and protection is that?
Still, we are falsely led to believe that most of the officers are good, and that it's just a few corrupt police officers that are ruining it for the whole.

I say if there are no good citizens, there are certainly no good police! If indeed every citizen has the potential to be corrupt, every police officer has a higher potential to be so
because of the power that's in their hands and the fact that they are also citizens that took an oath to be police,
They weren't born police.
Every crime is a crime,
even if it is a police officer, he or she is a criminal.
However, when an ordinary citizen wrongs another citizen or violates the law, the police come and arrest the parties considered guilty. They read them their Miranda rights, tell them they are innocent until proven guilty in the court of law, and take them to jail.

Suspicious citizens are often arrested if the police feel they are an accessory to the crime. Anyone considered to be withholding evidence or information can be arrested for obstruction of justice.

So, we are bamboozled by a system that allows police to commit crimes daily as the officer's band together in unity to cover for one another. Then they falsely believe their actions are not a complete obstruction of justice and that they are not criminals.
Wow! What a false belief!

Falsely we believe
that we are the most powerful and most exceptional nation in the world, while we seek allies to join us in attacking a supposed weaker nation. We now owe other countries so much money that America can't afford to pay it back.

We falsely believe that the President of the United States is the most powerful man in the world but not one President has been able to bring the world together in peace or even get the Republicans and the Democrats to be on the same page. So, falsely we believe that the United States are genuinely united while we have the Red States and Blue States and the Independent States that pledge to agree to disagree, yet not be disagreeable. Republicans and Democrats are always at odds with each other. Blacks and whites are under the red, white, and blue because anti-discrimination and anti-segregation put them together. So, people are led to believe that blacks and other minorities are treated as equals to whites living in America. What a great fallacy!

Falsely we believed that the elimination of Jim Crow laws were the ultimate victory and triumph.
That only made racist white Americans more sophisticated in their campaign. They camouflaged their hearts with smiles and greetings while continuing in their white privilege and superior white mentality with microaggressions. Wearing black robes and police uniforms and everyday attire, they continue to pervert justice and frustrate equality. Why is it so readily believed that a badge makes a peace officer? That a briefcase means integrity? That a black robe indicates justice? Or that gold teeth and dreadlocks indicate thugs? Why are Americans so foolishly ready to believe that any one of these things give credence to anyone's character? Is it because we don't know what to believe? Is it because Americans have been misled for so long that we think that all we must hold onto is our nation's false beliefs?

Falsely we believe that democracy will work for every country in the world when in many cases it's not even working for us.
Yes, falsely we believe that the tragedies and atrocities
we see and hear of are the losses and sorrows of others,
however, accept it or not, we are all in that family.
How long will we continue to falsely believe?

"The tragic reality," continued the Wise Man, "is that America has been falsely led for centuries. And instead of doing all within our power to make things better for everyone, many Americans are still standing around with the attitude of 'well, it's not my fault or my business. And I can't help anyway,' they say. But, shouldn't we realize by now that we are all brothers and sisters? Uniquely bound together because we are all in the human family. Therefore, we are all a part of the losses and setbacks. The tragedies, the problems and disasters of others in the adjoining room, directly or indirectly indeed affect us all. Furthermore, unless we come together in this land of supposed freedom, we will all be sailing in an enormous Titanic, and we'll all be devastated more severely than the MS Estonia."

The Wise Man coughed, took a sip of water and continued. "One of the most devastating false beliefs in the world is the concept of the white race being the superior race. This is a very strong delusion and a very entangling lie. Consequently, whites are in bondage to the very thing they accepted as their badge of greatness, their symbol of honor. Now they are serving the lie they embraced because they put on the garment of superiority, and superiority can never have an equal nor does it get a day off! In addition, the day they accepted the loftiness of superiority, they declared themselves to be gods among men, as they simultaneously declared all other races would have to settle for being mere humans."

"In North America, whites have been taught the entangling lie so long that it's almost like second nature. It's not that they go around saying to themselves or to others, "I'm superior, I'm entitled!" but it's the entire system that has been set up around white privilege, white superiority, and white entitlement, that has corrupted the whole. This white superiority mentality and the white privilege ideologies embraced by many whites has given false realities and false identities to white Americans, and false identities and false realities were given to the minorities in America by them, especially to blacks and Latinos. And, even if every white does not agree with the concept or fall for the lie, white entitlement benefits them, so they use the privilege."

The Wise Man looked very concerned and continued his thoughts. "After our forefathers allowed the system of corruption in this land, sadly, they were compelled to cater to it. So, they inadvertently or purposefully placed a higher godship on American whites, which has been their flag throughout the generations. However, that false ideology and false identity placed American whites in a stronger bondage, one that they may not know they are in. Subsequently, in every generation, white Americans are chained to their false badge of superiority and linked to the duplicity of white entitlement."

"Think about this," he said exhaling slowly, "The 'African-American,' as they have been named, have been called predators, super predators, threats to society, thugs, monkeys, (the N-word) and many other derogatory names or terms that you have heard. These thoughts are still alive in America today. And, until these views completely change, and white Americans denounce their superiority as a race, do away with their microaggressions, stop labeling blacks as threats, and truly see blacks and other ethnicities as equals, white Americans can never be free. And blacks and other minorities will keep being mistreated and mistrusted."

The Wise Man sighed and continued. "Have you noticed? The narrative for white Americans is quite different than the narrative used to describe minorities. Have you noticed? Every February we go back down slavery lane and revisit black people being enslaved, all the way to the Emancipation Proclamation and the Civil Rights movement. And while recognizing the people who have helped America is tremendous and inspiring, we must learn from what we had progression. The vicious cruelties of whites who held slaves and the mean and evil things that whites practiced for many years are never emphasized in the history books. Why must we wait until February to recognize the horrible treatment of blacks and to learn how they were used? Is it that whites don't want to be seen in that horrific light? Or is that they don't want to see their ancestors as such cruel and inhumane people with all that ugly, demeaning, superiority!"

The Wise Man closed his eyes moaned and continued.
"Do you realize the campaign against certain foreigners, especially Mexicans is getting worse? Why are the underlying concepts that rule America's thinking always pro-white, not pro-American? Have you noticed this?" asked the Wise Man rhetorically. "I have and it saddens me, because believe it or not, it's a terrible prison Caucasians have put themselves in.

Their prison of false beliefs and bias is dangerous," he said frowning and shaking his head slowly, "because at its core, it is an ungodly spirit's influence. Therefore, the prison that whites have created for themselves may be far worse than the slavery they forced on others."

"Therefore, I hope you can see that white entitlement and white superiority is a system of corruption and a snare. And the white leaders of the past that accepted this system of imbalance, that is still being followed by many now, is a system that God despises. God never intended for whites to treat blacks or other ethnicities so cruelly. God never intended for any man to rule another man unfairly. God never sees any race of people as superior to another. So, when America claims, "in God we trust," and we are following God, what God are we referring to? Because the intent of the one true God is always for people to love each other and be fair. Nevertheless, the good 'ole boy leaders, who set up the good 'ole boy network, don't want anyone to let go of the idol they embrace because that idol gives them power and keeps black and white Americans at odds. It keeps America in an undercurrent of turmoil. So, I repeat," said the Wise Man sorrowfully, "white Americans are often slaves to their ideology and others are abused by it. And as long as white entitlement exists in America, Americans cannot declare this is a land of equality."

One listener, with much agitation in his voice said, "What makes you think you're the authority on wisdom? And what makes you feel you have it all figured out when it comes to white Americans? Or America in general?"

"I never said I was, and I never said I do," replied the Wise Man. "As a matter of fact, I never insinuated it, nor implied in any way that my wisdom exceeded anyone else's knowledge in this roo-"

"Well," the listener interrupted. "Let me finish," said the Wise Man. "I'm not sure if you were here earlier when I had begun, but I did express directly or at least indirectly that I don't consider myself by any means to be more intelligent or wiser than any of you. I would dare to say there are quite assuredly several people in this room that are by far more intelligent than I. However, the point remains, I was asked to share my experiences and my views, and they most certainly will not match in perfect harmony everyone's opinions gathered today. Nevertheless, I was invited to speak, I had given an open invitation to all, and you decided to stop by!"

"Well, I don't agree with your views," stated the man aggressively with acrimony in his voice and posture.

"That is your right as a person, and it's your constitutional right also," said the Wise Man. "I know my rights," he replied angrily. "And I don't agree with you," he continued. "America is the greatest nation in the world! The greatest country in the WORLD!", he emphasized. "And I also think you're a stereotypical, egotistical butthead!" he said through somewhat gritted teeth and blaring eyes that could have sawed the Wise Man in half.

"America has done many great things," the Wise Man replied to his comments. "And my debate is not to prove or disprove its place in the history of great nations. However, America set its sails in the wrong direction a few centuries ago and has followed that sad path into its present state. It is a beautiful country, but the forefathers stagnated its overall greatness with the promotion of whiteness and the degradation of blacks. It put a great divide in its core structure. Furthermore, it trapped white Americans that never held that view of superiority; they are targets of misconception through guilt by association and are often looked at strangely by their own race because of their views."

"I don't have to listen to you," the agitated man stated. "This generation of white Americans doesn't have anything to do with slavery." "That may be true," responded the Wise

Man. "However, this generation of white Americans are still reaping the benefits of what was done in the past and what's done presently while present-day black Americans are still facing the struggles of inequality and brutality. Blacks receive stricter sentences, are treated crueler in arrest situations, are often viewed as threats, have never received an apology for the atrocities committed against them as a people, and are scrutinized in ways unimaginable to fellow citizens of the white race in every aspect of our society."

The psychological, economic and social benefits in America that whites enjoy just by being white, blacks have never known that luxury or convenience. Furthermore, the "40 acres, a mule and $100" that the American government promised blacks, ask a black person has anyone in their family ever received it? Where's the reparations for the crimes and mutilation committed against the black race?"

"So, you don't have to listen," said the Wise Man frankly, "but until we look at this truth in the face together as Americans and choose another path, we will forever be sweeping the real issues under the rug. We should all get on our knees if you ask me! So, if you are offended, it wasn't my deepest intentions. Though, I did say that some of you would probably be agitated by the truth shared."

Many heads were nodding in agreement and a few began to clap their hands. The big burly guy commented, "We came to hear you share your life and experiences, so you might as well finish!" He continued, "We might not agree with or like all that the Wise Man says, but at least we can show him the courtesy of listening. Besides, we can leave if we want, he's not holding us hostage." The burly guy looked around the room as if to say, do you all agree with this? The nods began again. There were a few annoyed people, and some angry faces mingled in the crowd, and some left the room, but most seemed in agreement. "Thank you," the Wise Man said, with a courteous smile, "thank you all very much!" The Wise Man waited until the crowd was settled and began ...

Dark Days

Dark days flooded America.
Racism was revealed and equality died.
Hate, greed, or fear moved in the land
or maybe all three moved in unison
upon the fathers
for they sadly moved away from the fundamental beliefs.
The constitution was violated, then assaulted
and blood began soaking America's soil.
White prejudice and white superiority had begun its course.
white privilege was moving steadily forward,
America was moving foolishly backward.
Could they not hear the constitution?
pleading with them in agony,
begging them not to destroy their brothers
whose blood was as red as theirs and
whose dreams were as real as theirs only different.
Theirs were dreams of liberty, equality, equity,
and the chance to keep their dignity, sanity,
and their families together.
But they were separated,
sold, degraded, hated by their white brothers
whose pride-filled prejudice
embraced the thought of supremacy.
But all men are brothers from the same earthly mother,
not the Big Bang Theory, or grandiose evolution.
All start from Eve,

and are conceived as sons to be equal.
But these sons left the lands of Europe,
donned red white and blue coats,
established themselves in colonies and
then stole the land from the red man
and then enslaved the black man
to work the land, they had taken.
Could they not hear equality crying out for justice?
When people forget all men are equal,
the system of separation dominates and creates havoc;
by destroying other humans
people eventually destroy themselves.
When whites separated black people
they could not see they were dividing white people as well.
When whites belittled blacks, they dishonored themselves
and stagnated the chances of this great nation being greater.
The constitution was in their heads
but absent from their hearts!
They upheld the constitution in theory but not in practice.
Sadly, whites hurting blacks were unconsciously displaying the brutality within themselves while they called black's savages.
And the saddest reality is that their ideology
keeps them from genuinely progressing.
For no man can fully demonstrate equality, equity, justice,
while displaying unfairness towards another!

"Hatred, pride, and arrogance plus beliefs of superiority are destructive to any people," said the Wise Man as he made a fist.

"Hatred, pride, and arrogance eat at the interior of society and will not let it develop to its full potential. When a nation lacks equality, it becomes imbalanced, and all the pseudo justice cannot patch the seams that are guaranteed to rip. The only way a country can genuinely declare greatness is when there is liberty and justice for all. When there is a correct balance in its system for rich and poor, male, and female, black and white, plus all colors in between, then they can declare true greatness!"

Someone in the audience shouted somewhat melodically, "That's the truth!" Another shouted, "I agree. It's time for a change in America. We can't continue following America's imbalanced path." Someone in the middle of the room shouted, "Passion, that's what America needs now; not just any 'ole passion either, but a great passion for unity and fairness among all our people. We need love so deep and concerted among the masses for unity that it silences the voices of the racist, of the haters, of the greedy capitalists, and of the whites that have used their privilege to the disadvantage or hurt of others." He continued, "Americans need to pledge allegiance to Christ, and to one another, more than to the flag! We need to stop white privilege and white entitlement so that everyone will be equal! Does that make sense to anyone else?"

The young white male with jeans and a white t-shirt had begun his declaration."Sir," he said to the Wise Man, I absolutely understand your point. Unless we come together in fairness in America, we will at some point self-destruct. Our country is imploding around us! That's the history of every great nation. Destruction in its interior before the enemies from without!" The young man then said, "Here's my pledge! I pledge allegiance to my brothers and sisters,
black, white, and all colors in between

to do all I can to respect and treat them as I want to be treated. I pledge not to be biased or prejudiced and not to target any group and mistreat them merely because of their ethnicity. I pledge to see all people as equals and treat them as such. And I pledge to not use white privilege to the advantage of myself and the disadvantage of others now that I have looked the tyrant in the face."

The Wise Man was almost speechless. The young man had declared volumes with his statement. A broad and gracious smile covered the Wise man's face. "Let's give this young man a round of applause." There was cheering in the room and a subtle wave of brightness was circling from person to person. There was a breath of transition like the beginning of autumn when the leaves start to fall or the essence of spring when the blooming begins. Breaking the air, the Wise Man said calmly but with power, "Listen! Listen!"

For All

A word
is just a word
until its meaning is
comprehended or lived.
Ideas
are just ideas
until
they are set in motion.
Water
becomes polluted
when it ceases movement
such as equality and liberty.
denied or withheld from any individual.
Remains JUST A WORD
Remains JUST AN IDEA
is JUST STAGNANT WATER.

"This young man has given us a beautiful picture painted with words. It's definitely the picture I'm striving to portray each day. I find that honesty is one of the hardest pieces of bread to swallow, yet it is the most nutritious for our souls," stated the Wise Man. One woman joined in and hollered, "I'd rather a big bowl of bitter honesty and grainy truth over spoons of sugary lies that taste so well but decay our souls and ruin our lives in the long run."

Reality had been presented, and it seemed everyone was ready for the hurt and healing that truth brings with it. "In the land of hypocrisy," began the Wise Man, then paused, closed his eyes and tilted his head to the side and straightened it out again. He opened his eyes and raised his hand as if he was about to wave at someone in the crowd, then he adjusted his shirt sleeve and lowered his arm again. He spoke slowly and deliberate, enunciating his words with emphasis.

In the Land of Hypocrisy

In the land of hypocrisy, the stakes are always high.
There we'll watch the trusting followers and the blind leaders wobble down a strange path together where criticism is frequent, recidivism often, and the combination of words coupled with equality in their corresponding actions are seldom ever heard of. There, folk swear by God and act like the devil, speak of responsibility and act irresponsibly, set up laws and violate justice, preach of purity and live in secret sin, speak of exceptional standards and openly live beneath them.
In the land of hypocrisy, there is danger. The policeman is a father. The teacher is a mother. The preacher is an uncle. The judge is a grandfather. And they are all trusted by someone who believes in them. Their choices place them in the same puzzle in one way or another. Their decisions make them the same in one way or another, especially if they are hypocritical in their actions.

It's absurd that hypocrisy is so prevalent in our culture and that it has positioned itself in every level of society.

What's illegal for those in poverty or the less fortunate, is allowed for the rich and powerful. Politician's lie, cheat and manipulate the very laws they say they stand for and when they are caught red-handed doing something illegal, it's tidily swept under the rug. Then, taxpayers inadvertently fund their misdeeds because the politician still gets a check each month.

It's the same scenario for most police officers who commit heinous crimes caught on camera; they go on leave with pay. The family hurt by their actions goes on unpaid grief for life. So, that also goes for any judge that's sentencing individuals for a misdemeanor or felony, and then excuses their family member who commits a felony or misdemeanor or gives a crooked cop a pardon is a hypocrite and a gross perverter of justice. I don't want to hear about another priest or pastor practicing the sins they tell us not to commit. And furthermore, I'm fed up with people complaining about boys with their pants sagging. They say, "These boys don't have any respect." That's right, they should pull their pants up because it is disrespectful. But when a finger pointer is a person who is doing something just as ridiculous, but is not as pointed out by society, he or she is hypocritical and judgmental.

One of the most hurtful and sad cases of hypocrisy comes from women who belittle women who have several children from different men but cover up the fact that they had an abortion or aided someone who had one. So, what shall we do when our lives are on display and the eyes that are watching and observing those lives are being confused by the poor examples, they see which don't match the words they hear? Like the parent that tells their child to lie about their age at a restaurant and then reprimands the child when that same child lies to them about something else.

How shall we teach the children to stop doing what we practice before them? How shall we hold others accountable for things we are secretly or openly doing ourselves?

The expectations are always high in the land of hypocrisy. In that strange and deceptive land, the hypocrite's fingers keep pointing out other people's shortcomings, as well as their inabilities, while spotlighting the standard of their uprightness and ethical judgments. Like Pharisees, they say pull those pants up! I say be careful that our character is not sagging lower than the boy's pants that need pulling up. Because in the land of hypocrisy, the stakes are always high, and every day reveals how easy it is to become a hypocritical pharisee, pointing out the splinter in someone's eye while having a plank in your face.

Once again, the Wise Man had shaken some leaves off of the autumn trees! Everyone including himself was persuaded to look at themselves and evaluate if that pertained to them. Retrospection was also a challenge. The Wise Man had merely placed reality like a mirror in everyone's hands and allowed them to look in it. The mirror was clear of any ambiguity or muddle and the simplicity of the truth had done that. So, his intent was not to point fingers; he was simply challenging them with the truth! He had done precisely as the lady had suggested; he had given big bowls of bittersweet honesty.

"Would you agree," he said "that America the beautiful has been gripped by hypocrisy? America seems to be under controlled chaos and winking at it, as a grandfather casually dismissing his grandchild's rude behavior, that won't make things better. My heart is saddened as I look around and watch this country spiral into more confusion under our current leaders. It's repulsive when our leaders tell blatant lies, and those lies are switched into statements, such as, "They're fact challenged or it's just fact misrepresentation, by the hypocritical liars defending them." The Wise Man shook his head in a languid motion demonstrating his distaste. "Hypocrisy and blatant lies in all levels, in all levels," he repeated sadly. "Yes! America's struggle is, unfortunately, very real! And it doesn't matter if it's the left wing, right wing or all wings combined, pushing hypocritical and devious agendas because the end effect is hurtful for Americans." The Wise Man took another sip of water, moved his body forward and said …

What's Your Next Move?

I've watched America move from good sense to nonsense,
from common sense to no-sense,
from prayer in school to corruption in school,
from sanity to insanity;
from love to hate,
from pride to just being prideful,
from blacks having no rights to civil rights
and back again to clandestine slavery.
America moved from morals to immorality,
from subtle drug use to obvious drug use,
to an epidemic of drug addiction,
from semi-governmental effectiveness to arguing political correctness,
from constitutional rights to constitutional fights
won by him that best manipulates the constitution,
and from being a lender to being a borrower,
from being over the dragon
to being almost entirely owned by the dragon,
from shaking a bear to being in cahoots with the bear.
America, America, God shed his grace on thee
America, America, God showed his face to thee
America, America, what's it going to be?
What's your next move?
America, the land of milk and honey, but the milk
tastes sour and the honey is hard to find.
America, the land of no child left behind

yet many of America's children never move further than
moving from the conventional oven to the microwave oven,
or from the home-cooked dinner to the TV dinner.
America, how did we move from grownups raising children,
to children raising children, and in many cases,
children telling their parents what to do?
America, how did we get to the place of being in a constant
hurry? Rush, rush, rush! And continual worry?
Stress, stress, stress!
Where did the turn take place?
To talking a lot and saying too little?
America, how did we move from living
day to day, to not really living at all?
What happened to the days of leaving our house door unlocked?
Why do many public schools look like jails?
Shouldn't the local church resemble Jesus?
Where is the old family structure,
and what happened to the handshake that sealed an agreement?
The handshake that did not require contracts and lawyers
to verify it was real and legitimate?
America, where's our integrity?
America, what's our motive?
America, what's our intention?
America, what's our direction?
America, where are we going from here?
Shall we keep this course or chart a new one,
or perhaps just return to ethical values?
America, has misused liberty become your entrapment?
America, America, God shed his grace on thee
America, America, God showed his face to thee
America, America, what's it going to be?
What's our next move?

Rising from his position from the edge of the seat, he adjusted his shirt sleeves again and continued with emphasis, "That's the question in the minds of many Americans, what do we do? Where do we go from here? How do we fix the problems that we face as a nation from day to day, from moment to moment?" The Wise Man looked around the room in amazement and said, "America is a beautiful land, and the American people are strong and beautiful people in many ways." He cleared his throat and continued, "It rose from the tyranny of England and became a dominant force almost overnight in comparison to other great nations and kingdoms before it. It's only been in existence a few centuries and a couple of decades, and yet in that time it rose to enormous prominence."

"I sincerely believe," stating with an emphasis, "that America was sidetracked because of the social and racial inequalities that they promoted since the beginning formation of America."

"Maybe the quick rise to the forefront caused internal dizziness like vertigo. Perhaps it was the fear of the future that caused the forefathers to make the terrible choices they made. Or, perhaps a few secret societies have intoxicated our land to delirium and the outcome of their deliberate misguidance has been exposing itself over the years and the masses are crying for a doctor. But, no one was allowed to rush America to the emergency room because a select few have always benefitted from America's drunkenness, sickness and division. Therefore, they wanted America to stay stuck. Racism benefits them, white privilege, poverty, and other social imbalances from A to Z benefit the select few more than it does the whole that are being used by their scheme so, pulling the entire group out of the hole would defeat their purpose."

"I can relate to that thought," interjected the lady who previously said, "Give me bowls of truth. I can see it clearly." "America is a product of misguided perspective! Of selective and suggestive reasoning, of subluminal concepts projected on our minds by the propaganda machine and those with power agendas. Wow! We've become one-eyed midgets," she said laughing thoughtfully.

"Exactly!" remarked the Wise Man. "That's where America is, and unless we start to look at things through different eyes, with both eyes open, healing is impossible. Everyone must grab their ego, their pride, their prejudice, their white privilege, their blindness to propaganda, and whatever other negative force is holding America hostage and throw it as far from them and us as possible. As Americans, we must ask God to give us love for each other. Genuine Christ-like love for each other if it's really in God we trust! Plus, a realistic view of ourselves and the powers behind the corruption in America."

"Unless we pledge allegiance to God and to one another as the young man said, how shall we make it as a nation? Consider this," said the Wise Man as calmly as possible.

The Inside Man

Just as destructive as what man does
to another human
is what he does to himself.
Since out of the heart
proceeds the things which defile the man,
a person's ill thoughts
and actions towards another person
makes them a nation crumbling from within.
Liars lie. Cheaters cheat. Thieves steal.
Rude people are impolite, greedy people are covetous,
cruel people are not kind, etc.
So, what man does is what he has become.
Therefore, a person's self is his greatest obstacle.
A person's self is his greatest opponent.
Man's conscious wars are against himself
It's the voice that he must shut out.
It's the voice he's determined to silence.
It's the opponent that he must overcome.
And even when man sears his own conscious
and hardens his heart to the truth
that stares him in his face,
time and time again
in the vast corridors of man's mind,
in the broad hallways of man's reasoning,
or just in a quiet corner of man's thoughts,
the conflict will arise.

The harsh beast of reality will confront him
because man has a tough time
getting completely away from himself.
Even if he convinces himself that he's not the issue,
nor a part of the problem,
at some turn or intersection, he'll bump into himself,
the real man in the mirror that goes with him everywhere.

"I say, therefore, we must make the necessary adjustments to have a better mindset. We are all connected in the family of humanity. So, we must put away our differences and find our common ground; that place where we are joined by biology and then be governed by love and harmony because we all share the same blood, and unity gives strength. But we must be careful not to join in destructive unity. Destructive unity is when we join together for the wrong purpose. Any unity among people that hurts other people without proper cause is destructive unity."

"Then, as we join in unity that is not destructive, we must also choose to forgive each other. Forgiveness is a potent tool; it releases both the forgiver and the forgiven from any further carrying of the past and cancels all debts. To forgive means 'one does not hold the other in debt any longer for any offenses committed.' In that moment of forgiveness, liberty is extended, and bondage can never take place in the heart of he who forgives; it's impossible!"

The Wise Man smiled again and continued, "You may say to yourself, forgiving them doesn't change how they are; they'll still be greedy, selfish, unkind people on power trips and do all the things they always did. My forgiveness won't take their purse strings away, or cause them to be fair, or topple their corrupt system. It probably won't do any of those things I just named but it will give you peace with God. And peace with God is more important than all the money or power that corrupt society holds."

"Peace with God changes things dramatically. It makes people search themselves and then extend themselves with the thought of unity governed by love. Do you realize unity can never grow where division lives; and holding unforgiveness in one's heart brings a more severe wound to the offended than the offense does. It's clear America is sliding downhill, and we don't know how far it's going to slide, and yes, it started a long time ago. However, it doesn't help by throwing rocks or adding gas to the fire. A desire to see America do better should be in the heart of every American and it should be the position of every Christian to pray for America because it's in desperate need of God's help."

He joined his hands together intertwining his fingers and raised them over his head like an arc. "I pray," he continued, "that we can learn as Americans to love each other. As we pardon our offenders, we should also repent for staying on the road of foolishness as a nation for so long. We should be covering each other as family not looking for ways to destroy each other like enemies."

"Why don't we let love the noun, love the adjective, and love the verb guide us in every area of our lives; then we can do better. And, if we are willing to surrender to the Lord, He can bring about the most significant transformation possible. As a nation, we must change how we do things, how we look at things! Especially how we look at and treat each other! Love, forgiveness and unity build an arch." He lowered his arms and put his hands in front of his face. "pride, arrogance, greed, entitlement, and unforgiveness all build individual walls and are even worse when combined. Have you ever considered that?" the Wise Man asked.

How We See It

Perspective
will make the difference
between
Yes. No.
Fast. Slow.
Stay. Go.
What's a priority?
And what's secondary?
What's
Meaningful or meaningless,
What to ignore or what to address
when we move or stay stationary.
What's right or wrong,
what's wrong or right
does not change just the light
by which they are viewed, but
gives a reflection,
of that person's point of view,
of that person's position, too.
Recognizable
by his or her perspective.

"So, we can conclude," continued the Wise Man, "the necessity of developing a better perspective of each other in America is imperative for our forward progress. Unless our attitudes change, neither shall we! It will be just a thought! Just an idea! Just stagnant water!"

"There was an ant that climbed the same tree every day," said the Wise Man. "Not only did it climb that same tree, but it climbed it the same way every day, straight up the middle. At the top of that tree was a wise owl, which the ant would visit from time to time. One day, as the owl and the ant were talking, the ant said, "Nothing changes. It's always the same. You're always the same. I'm always the same. This tree and our surroundings are always the same. The same! The same! The same!"

"Why do you feel this way?" questioned the owl curiously. "Because it's true," said the ant assertively. "I see," said the owl tilting its head a little to the left and observing the ant inquisitively. "Have you considered perhaps that it's your view that's stuck, not the things around you?" asked the owl. "My view?" said the ant, a bit offended. "My view?" "Perhaps," said the owl. The Wise Man continued his illustration. "Maybe the things around you are changing, but in your mind, because you have decided all is stale and stagnant, you overlook it." "No, I don't think so," replied the ant. "Nothing is changing; it's all the same. "May I challenge you?" asked the owl, "Tomorrow climb this tree from the other side and look again. It will be the same tree," stated the ant assuredly." "It will be the same tree," said the owl, "but perhaps you'll understand it better tomorrow."

The ant scurried down the tree with the thought of proving the wise owl wrong and couldn't wait until the next day to express his victory. That morning, it climbed the tree from the back side upward to the owl's nest.

"Good morning," he greeted the owl very energetically. The owl returned the greeting, then asked, "What did you see?" "The same thing from the other side," replied the ant in a triumphant tone of voice." "Exactly!" said the owl, "Exactly?" questioned the confused ant. "Yes, exactly," stated the owl once more, "because you didn't change your inner view, the world around you didn't either! Now, adjust your outlook and perspective, and your world can change also!"

"Holdup!" said the ant to the owl, a bit defensive. "What you're trying to tell me is that all I need to do is change my view, and everything can change?" "Precisely!" responded the owl. "The attitude and perspective of any person affect every aspect of their life and everything they encounter. Think about it," said the owl to the ant. "It's impossible to be negative and spread positives. It's impossible to harbor hate and spread love. It's impossible to hold unforgiveness in one's heart and be kind. It's impossible to have a lousy view of someone and see them in a good light. Shall I continue?" asked the owl. "No," said the ant. "I think I get it. But, is it really that simple? questioned the ant thoughtfully. "Yes, it is really that simple," replied the owl. "When our view changes and we begin to see ourselves, others, and the world around us in a better light, things become more bearable and our lives become much brighter."

"That doesn't mean we cover up reality and pretend that there is nothing wrong in this world. Nor does that mean we should allow things that need changing in our society to remain the same and not challenge them."

"I don't mean that at all," said the owl very pointedly. "We must face the things we encounter, but we must meet them with the right point of view. Do you see what I mean?" asked the owl. "Yes, I do," the ant replied and crawled down the tree with a new perspective.

The Wise Man finished his illustration and repeated "Therefore, unless our perspectives change, neither shall we. It will be just a thought! Just an idea! Just stagnant water!"

"Personally," said the Wise Man, "and I do mean very personally, a few of my friends and associates had a discussion when I was younger because we were gravely concerned with what we could do to help make society and ourselves better seeing how society had pegged and labeled us. We recognized that if you want to see a change in anyone else, you should begin with yourself. We thought about the opportunities ahead and the difficulties we would face. We didn't let anything discourage us, in spite of the troubles that followed; we just moved on and steadily moved forward."

"We made our decision that we would make our mark no matter what! No matter how small, it would still be a mark made with indelible ink on the pages of our culture. Perhaps the masses wouldn't know our hearts or our stand, but everyone that we engaged with or interacted with would most assuredly realize that we had decided to soar as high as our wings could carry us. We would go the extra mile. Just like Jesus said, 'If they ask you to go one mile, go two.' Our thought was, why not give it a try before they ask, realizing the challenge was already facing us."

The Wise Man cleared his throat and carried his views forward. "Going the extra mile ain't no joke; it's often doing and giving more without getting or receiving pay, support, recognition, or anything for that matter." Rubbing his hands together, he continued his thoughts.

"If you go the extra mile, you will often be going alone. There are not many travelers on that road. The way is a little too far and most times a little too difficult for the egotistical person or the self-centered folks that can't see beyond their views. Not many have the will or the determination for it. Not many have the unselfishness required to journey the rugged path of the extra mile. Some give up at the line of, 'I've done my job,' others stop at the edge of, 'It's not my responsibility, and it's not my concern or my problem,' so why should I be giving any extra effort? Why should I be concerned with them at all? Have you ever felt like that?" he asked, glancing briefly at each face of the listeners.

"Often times, people throw in the towel when they wonder what they will receive for their extra effort. Their mind can't digest the idea of doing anything extra for the benefit of someone else while thinking this won't be beneficial for them. That voice in their head hammers them with the echoing tune of 'What's in it for me?' won't stop playing, so they walk out after starting or they don't start out at all! You've seen them before," said the Wise Man. "The takers! The users! The abusers! The egotistical! The self-centered! They occupy every walk of life. For example, at the job they're hawks watching the time clock. They spend more energy figuring out ways not to do work than it would take to do the work and get it over with."

"They're vacuums, sucking in as much as they can, while putting in as little effort as possible. They're mastering their skills daily. They're takers and when they give, it's with an ulterior motive. And while you do the work, they'll be paid just like you, sometimes more!"

"I hear you!" hollered a man from the gatherers. "Man, do I hear you! The extra mile is a lonely place," continued the Wise Man. "You'll be labeled and eyed with scrutiny by other workers. Sometimes you'll lose a few colleagues if your motivation magnifies their lackadaisical work ethic. Occasionally, you'll be mocked if you're not willing to be scrupulous. Some will squint at you with eyes of tyranny, and sneer when you walk past them. 'Who does he think he is? She thinks she's all that!' they say under their breath, or just loud enough for you to hear it as they comment to each other while sipping coffee in the lounge."

The Wise Man continued, "I genuinely believe not going the extra mile has caused quite a few setbacks in society."

"If the founding fathers of America had gone an extra mile to make sure freedom and justice was for all in the early years of our nation, and if the beautiful South would have gone an extra mile to abandon their system of injustice, and the North, East and West would have made it a concerted effort to practice equality, unity would truly exist in America today."

"Families have been torn apart, friendships have been ruined, marriages have folded, and nations have crumbled because going the extra mile takes endurance and kindness, selflessness and patience, plus the determination to not give up, and not throw in the towel."

"The extra mile mentality is this," stated the Wise Man, and as if by metamorphosis, he appeared to have sprouted wings when he said, "I shall give my best to be my best at everything I do. I shall be willing to help whoever I can whenever I can, regardless of their race, creed, or culture. I will continuously give my best effort to be an agent of positive change striving to leave conditions better after I depart than they were when I arrived. And, if with all my efforts, I cannot leave a person or a place in a better state, may I never leave it in a worse one due to my actions or lack of them. That is the extra mile mentality! In your home! At your job! In your life! So, I repeat, the extra mile 'ain't no joke!' but the extra mile is definitely worth the trouble!"

The Wise man smiled, shifted his body slightly and said, "You may inquire or make the statement, 'What about the people that go an extra mile in a negative way?' The individuals that will climb on everyone's head to get what they want and then stand on everyone's shoulders to stay there. What about them? Well, my only suggestion is recognizing them for who they are and doing your best not to aid them in their pursuits."

"Excuse me! Excuse me sir!" said a listener, appearing a bit disgruntled. "My name is Pal Suoreficov, and I want to make sure that I've heard you correctly." "Concerning what?" said the Wise Man curiously. Pal responded that many people go the extra mile for selfish reasons." "I didn't say 'many,' but yes, I made a similar statement," replied the Wise Man. "Did you also say," asked Pal, "that America's primary motivations have been self-interest?" "In many ways, it has," the Wise Man replied calmly. Pal took a deep breath and continued, "If I heard you correctly, you stated many white Americans have used white privilege as a tool to their advantage."

The Wise Man nodded in agreement. Pal continued, "Even though they didn't fully agree with the unfairness of it, however, since it was more profitable for them to be quiet and go with the flow than to say anything and be scrutinized by other whites, they choose the easy road?"

"Yes," said the Wise Man. "I made that statement, not precisely in those words but yes, I did. And I meant it!" "Aren't you being judgmental in your views of white Americans?" Pal asked. "No!" replied the Wise Man, because the things that I've stated have indeed happened and no one can deny it. Pal responded sarcastically, "You need to leave this country if you don't like the way things are!" "Why would I go, and where?" countered the Wise Man. "I was born here. As I am sure, you were also. That makes us both Americans." Pal's words were icy. "You act like America is the worst place in the world, like white Americans have only done mean things and nothing else." "Not so," replied the Wise Man. "I simply recognize that America could be so much better if fairness were given to all citizens. That's my stand, what's yours?" asked the Wise Man. Pal frowned and didn't reply for a few seconds.

"I go the extra mile every day!" His words spewed out as if they had erupted from somewhere locked inside of him for decades. A volcano of emotions flowing out like lava, hot burning lava.

"I go the extra mile every day, and what has it brought me? Nothing! Absolutely nothing! Do you hear me?" he asked.

"I've been fair to blacks and whites because I see us as equals! We're all American! If we are born in this country, we are American! Yet my views haven't profited me, or my fairness. I've been called a liberal." He smirked and continued. "The extra mile has kicked me in the groin. My wife ran off with her boss! I can't see my kids! Her family treats me like I'm beneath them and I've never done anything to hurt them! I've never done anything to deliberately hurt anyone, black or white."

"So, the extra mile and all that stuff; save it, Sir," Pal stated while staring very intently at the Wise Man. "I have nothing against you, personally. But what you are saying sounds like hogwash and it's irritating. As you can all see," he said, shifting his gaze from the Wise Man to the gatherers and back again to the Wise Man. "I am WHITE! A white American! Has that benefited me? I've been passed over twice at my job, and the promotions I should have gotten were given to other people—once the guy I trained, and once to someone they brought into the company. And then the boss's cousin, Ronald Joe, came in and got paid more at entry level than I was getting after three years of employment. Nepotism at its finest!"

His disappointment had come out in angry spurts, and it was flowing hot and fast! In his frustration, he had not realized that he had just made a case and point illustration for the Wise Man, even if it was white on white unfairness. It was unfairness and a going of the extra mile in the wrong way!

"Believe me," said the Wise Man as kindly as possible, "The extra mile has costs, but it also has benefits. And, it will reward you someday. It may not seem like it will," the Wise Man explained, but it will reward you in time. In the meantime, remember greedy people are always selfish, egotistic people will make everything about them, and white privilege can never be fair; it was not designed to be," stated the Wise Man. "Therefore, as I said, try to identify them and don't aid them in their pursuits." The Wise Man shifted his eyes from Pal to the crowd and spoke again. "I once read some thoughts from J. H. Davis that relate to people like those Pal mentioned. Let me share his words with you, Mr. Davis said …"

Wild Thing

I recognize what you're trying to do to me.
You want me to work for free.
You're trying to change the nature in me
by clipping my wings.
I saw you watching and observing me.
As I soared high above you, I observed you pounding metal
into shackles and chains.
Look. There. See right over there, what is that?
Those burning pits that you're removing and placing in front
of my eyes are trying to blind me. Don't you know that that
will only make me not see?
I recognize what you're trying to do to me,
chaining and shackling my legs
to keep me from running free.
You're trying to change the nature of me.
You keep teaching me
in the ways that I will depend on you
while telling me, you need and depend on me.
Yeah, I recognize what you're trying to do to me;
you want me to work for free.
You're sneaking around my family,
turning my children against me;
now you even have my mother scolding me.
You imprisoned my father to brainwash me,
you're trying to change the nature in me.
Yeah, you want me to work for free!

The Wise Man paused, took a deep breath, and continued. "Power in its different methods and inventions is in the mentality of the greedy and self-centered person. That's their reality in a nutshell," glancing in Pal's direction, he continued. "They move some folks up and hold other folks down, but always to their own advantage."

"And even if they are not in a position of leadership,

they'll push and manipulate others, looking for an advantage for themselves. Their inspiration does not lead to fairness, and it's larger than just self-preservation. It's a drive pushing them like an addiction, like drugs or alcohol, so, everyone becomes a step to climb on or a step to stand on. It's an insatiable push! Anyone with power and no self-control, or greedy and selfish are like piranhas in a pool full of guppies."

"Some people's monsters are treacherous," he said while rubbing the back of his left ear. "I've often wondered," he said grinning seriously, "are they honestly happy? Do they have contentment and peace in their hearts, or is there deep unrest in their soul? How does their pillow really feel? What do they see when they close their eyes? These have been my questions for years," chuckled the Wise Man, showing concern. He moved slightly forward and looked around for a few seconds at the guests then spoke very frankly...

TagTeam Duo

Greed has many voices, and selfishness has many faces.
Each one of us has some of their traits in us,
so, if we give them our attention long enough, they may persuade us to follow their one-sided path.
Avoid those slippery places, stay out of those dark rooms,
for greed and egotism are smooth talkers;
they speak in confident tones.
Their words are powerful and seducing,
their speeches are well versed and rehearsed.
They'll implant a feeling of control and dominance in the recipient of their clamor.
Unfortunately, after they have planted their seed
and the roots have taken hold,
you will be impregnated with great partiality.
Afterward, you'll give birth to blinding prejudices
and overpowering unfairness.
This duo has ruined many men and lands
and caused great civilizations to stumble.
These two have gendered hate in humanities heart
and blackened humanity's perspective.
They have hardened the wills of men
and made them calloused and cold.
They have caused individuals and nations to become idolaters, fixated on themselves and the images they've erected.
These spirits keep them trapped in the labyrinth of self-interest
and wandering vainly in constant pursuit of temporal gains.

Do you want to be free? Stay away from selfishness and greed!
Don't give into their treachery!
Since greed has many voices and unfairness has many faces, and each one of us has a seed of their behavior in us,
we must be cautious not to birth and nurture their child."

The Wise Man paused and allowed the words he shared to take hold of his audience before he continued speaking. "We can be selfish and greedy in many ways. I unfortunately learnt the hard way that these are very clever devils, which can lead anyone down their path quicker than we want to believe possible."

"I am not exactly sure what drives greed, but I believe it's an unrestrained desire to get more. However, I'm thoroughly convinced selfishness is mostly connected to arrogance, insecurity, fear, greed, and a lack of trust in God. There may be other factors, but these stand out in my mind." The Wise Man half-smiled, wiped his face and continued.

"I realize that selfish people are not always greedy, but greedy people are always selfish. Just think about the combination in one person, that's a volatile mixture!" The Wise Man glanced around the room, observing the faces giving the listeners time to absorb his opinions and to express any views of their own. He allowed his gaze to scan their faces once more and began speaking again.

"Wouldn't it be wonderful if we could kill some of the negatives in our world just by talking about them, or by having an open discussion? That would be a plus," he said, "however, actions which correspond to what has been said always get the job done. Does anyone agree with that?" Several "I do's" and "yeses" sprinkled throughout the room.

The Wise Man's face became solemn as he spoke. "I've listened to, and I've heard about plenty of plans that went to the drawing board. I've sat in many conferences and on conference calls that were very energetic and exciting, but afterward, those suggestions laid inactive so long that those plans and talks are the definitions used in dictionaries next to the word dormancy. I've drudged through many discussions and strategies that should have been stopped before they even started." "Me too!" interjected several listeners. Others agreed with nods and slight smirks.

The Wise Man's face and demeanor were a picture of concern as he spoke. "It's easy to say we want to change things around us. It's easy to say we want better, but we must ask ourselves an earnest question—are we willing to change and do better? Am I concerned about the whole or am I just concerned with myself, is the question every person needs to ask themselves daily. Have you ever considered that most plans that people make cater to themselves and to a select few? This is an unfortunate reality, and it's very often the case of those in high positions."

"They sound good when they talk, they make it sound very appealing. Deceptive leaders will even add 'we' and 'us' several times when they speak. They often give the general public the impression that they are their primary concern. Rhetoric is an excellent tool to grab the minds of people who want to believe it. I know if you say something enough times and put the right twist and earworm on it, plus dress it in the proper attire, many people will be lured and trapped. And unfortunately, the propaganda machine always has enough puppets on staff to help them push their agenda."

"I'll give you an example. For years people have been saying, 'sticks and stones may break my bones, but words will never hurt me.' Well, you and I both know that words can do as much damage as sticks and stones, possibly even more. But, since it was said so many times and it had a good sound to it, perhaps we didn't give it the consideration and rational thought it should have gotten. On one side, it was meant to mean, 'No matter what you say, it won't affect me,' but what about the other meaning; the reality that words can hurt and hurt very deeply. What about the words being used to present a false view for manipulative purposes? Brainwashing words! Those words have a significant effect after their corresponding actions show the real face and heart of their deception. And, one thing is sure, the results of words used falsely for cunning purposes last a long time and do much damage. On the other hand, words coupled with positive actions help so much more, and that's true in every realm of society."

"Another thing I've noticed," said the Wise Man very seriously, "Self-deception is the worse deception of all because the lies we tell ourselves are the hardest to break away from. So, the deceived go around convincing themselves that they're right even when the foolishness of who and what they are following is pointed out. In their minds, those that don't share their views are fools; they would celebrate if you were to join their madness!

As previously stated, I'm concerned about society, our leaders and the path of our nation."

The Wise Man moved forward to be close enough to the edge of the podium. His passion was evident. "I'm very concerned," he said, looking around the room. "No, let me be as transparent as possible. I'm so troubled with us as people that it often breaks my heart and makes me want to shout. I am filled with a feeling of deep sorrow from all the disparaging things that are currently happening in our nation. It disturbs me how people can be so self-centered and how flippant our leaders handle the affairs of the nation at times. It's appalling how quickly they blatantly lie to the public and still want us to trust them. My heart goes out to America!" He was breathing deeply, and his gestures were now very animated. The gatherers looked in awe, surprise, or maybe with the same concern he had. Whatever the case, they all looked in his direction and added a few "yeses" here and there, and some said "Amen" as if they were a part of a revival that just happened to be at the Town Hall Center.

The Wise Man calmed down and regained his composure like an evangelist at the end of a sermon. Then he spoke with a somber expression on his face. "Conversations help at times, but actions will take us much further." Luana spoke from the crowd and said, "It is truly baffling how blind, cruel, and hurtful people can be." "True!" said another. "I agree," said Pal. "And nothing hurts more than when you are betrayed or hurt by people we trust." "Quite right," replied the Wise Man reflectively. "People can be so mean and stubborn that they lose sight of the bigger picture."

"If they're focusing on themselves, they won't see anything else. They're oblivious to cul-de-sacs and ditches because they feel those things don't pertain to them. And, if they happen to land in a ditch or drive to a dead-end, they won't take the blame for it, they'll point the finger at everyone but themselves."

"Some folks are so obstinate that bending or changing is not in their vocabulary. They represent thick 'ole trees that are no longer pliable, no longer flexible, and almost unreachable. They're forever rehearsing the good 'ole days and living there with enthusiasm and wanting society to continue doing the same. They know what they are doing is one-sided, yet they remain steadfast in their direction because it's more convenient than moving with change and giving a new way a chance. Many hard-hearted zealots of self-absorption don't believe they are wrong. They are adamantly biased in their ways of thinking, so it's easy for them to hold onto old beliefs and not move. It's sad but true. The cost is very high because now it has been generations of the same gloomy thing."

The Wise Man's eyes were ablaze and fiery as wood in a fireplace!

"I compare them," he said, "to a person jumping in a large pothole. They are trying to convince those who have started to go around it to jump back in it. They are trying to prove to everyone who has begun to assist their fellow citizens and family members to stay out of the hole that going back to it is better. They believe, and they want others to think that the good 'ole boy way is the best way and that the old ways of America which caused much grief is better than traveling together down the path of healing as a nation. They refuse to accept that pride, prejudice and an imbalanced social structure is always destructive to any nation. And that the very things that separate people and destroy nations are the wrong way to go."

"It seems to me," interjected Luana, "that it comes down to how, as a society, we want to be in the future." "That's about the size of it," sighed the Wise Man. "Change is always in our power, but unless we act upon it, everything will remain the same. So, please understand my words. Change only happens when you do. Listen to your heart and allow change to happen."

Then, with a fervent expression, he quoted Baruch Spinoza, "Sed omnia praeclara tam difficilia, quam rara sunt. This means, But all things excellent are as rare as they are difficult. So, I ask who's writing the lyrics and music to your song? Since your life is a melody and the people around you are listening to it, what sound and impression is being produced from your life? What type of tune is it? Are your words and life a harmonious composition or an off-beat cling and clang? Those were also the questions I asked myself," he smiled gently and continued.

Who's Writing the Lyrics to Your Song?

As I danced through life swaying to the rhythms and being driven by the melodies that I labored desperately to define and to understand, I often struggled to follow the directions of the director of the band.

I attempted to analyze the rhythm of the drumbeats and the runs of the bass; I was distracted by the mournful cry of the trombone and attracted to the soft whisper of the violins even though they saddened me.

The beckoning sounds of the flute and the melodic warnings of the saxophone encouraged me and the ear-shaking screams of the trumpet awakened me to the fact that I was writing lyrics to songs. In time, my spirit was troubled for little children were reading the lyrics to my songs.

A small voice reminded me that I was arrogant, self-serving, self-centered, puffed with lofty pride and full of conceit. The hands of time pointed me to my friend's home, to hear him teach, preach, pray, and sing with full conviction that God is almighty yet gentle, jealous yet understanding, chastising yet merciful. What began to amaze me is God gives us wealth, but we act impoverished! Health but we claim illness! And even if we're filled with envy, he provides us love, and despite his love, we're often filled with anger. He gives us joy, and we hold onto depression, comfort, and misery.

Nevertheless, when we stand, we never stand alone, for he never leaves or forsakes us, which leads me to ask who's writing the lyrics to your song?

I pray that God will define me in his image and that his grace and tender mercy will reflect in me for someone is still reading the lyrics to my song.

I thank God for those that are allowing me to read the beautiful lyrics of their song. And now I pose the question to every believer in the faith—who's writing the lyrics to your song? May God's blessings of perfect peace, joy, grace, love, and tender mercy continue with you all the days of your life and may you have wealth and health in the lyrics of your song.

The Wise Man seemed as animated as a fluttering butterfly. He looked like spirit in flight. His heart had been exposed and poured out like water or wine. He had made himself bare before them with his words and concerns. He trusted that those in attendance would realize that they were all transparent in the room because God could see them, and no one could hide from his vision, nor could anyone cover the music or their lyrics entirely from human observation, much less from God. "Everyone is always writing lyrics and making melodies with their lives, from day to day, from moment to moment," said the Wise Man. "The question is, what type of music do you want your life to reflect? What kind of song do you want your life to present? Realizing ...

Just Traveling Through

Our lives are a blend
of routines, practices, habits,
activities, and responsibilities,
performed daily
on the grand stage of life.
And,
as we progress toward the final curtain,
the unavoidable exit,
wouldn't it be comforting to know
that the habits we had,
the routines we followed,
the activities we were involved in,
the responsibilities we undertook,
and what we continuously practiced,
was not only good for us
but also beneficial for our contemporaries
and for our successors?
Since we are just traveling through,
wouldn't it be a pleasant compliment knowing
we honestly left a positive mark;
our permanent fingerprints,
pressed with indelible ink on the pages of time
which affected and shall affect
other's routines, practices, habits, activities,
and responsibilities.

"Who our lives affect and reflect, that's a sobering thought to consider," said the Wise Man very directly. "Our music, lyrics, and song, as well as habits, activities and responsibilities that connect us to people in one way or another are as waves of light or shadows of darkness that brighten or darken the world around us."

"That's very true," interjected Pal. The Wise Man continued, "Everyone's life is a symphony of those inner and outer melodies we make every day. So, we must try with all our energy to be a positive influence. I don't believe that individuals with good principles deliberately harm others, not like those who go the extra mile with their selfish intentions in mind as we discussed earlier. No, I cannot believe that. Most people with a stable moral structure want to make a beautiful melody with their lives. However, I firmly believe people with good intentions and morals sometimes find themselves with their back against the wall, feeling confined by the situation or circumstance and the pressure of other things, and they often react from that pressure instead of reacting from a place of peace."

"And, if there is no God peace in them, no God tranquility, and they don't know the more significant benefit of encountering troubles joyfully and walking through them with the Lord, they won't have balance when things get overly difficult no matter how good their intentions are. If gloom darkens the peace in them, if they are pushed or feel trapped entirely in the corner, the frustration often comes out blasting like a hurricane or volcano out of control. Furthermore, if the person or persons are living in the place of brokenness with past or present hurts, a lousy childhood, a resentful marriage, or any other broken relationship that is holding them psychologically captive or causing them the pain, they may go over the edge. The wounds in them may cause blunt words or actions that come out as being hurtful or harmful despite their moral beliefs or the desire to make positive life songs."

The Wise Man cleared his throat and continued. "Some people that feel they lacked opportunities or were cheated out of good breaks or were not successful when opportunities were presented and they become aggressive because of their feelings of insecurity, inability, or their view of society's unfairness. They have a sense of right and wrong and a passionate desire to be a positive role model. However, they've become discouraged because of the hand that life has dealt them or the way they played their hand. So, they begin struggling with their moral compass. It does not matter which group they fall into. The point is that people often act out of their place of hurt, not wholeness. They were not planning harm to others, but because they didn't know what to do with the injury or struggle inside themselves, they became hurtful. So hurt people sometimes tend to hurt other people but not necessarily with that intention; occasionally their routines, practices, and habits may just be out of sync."

"Have you ever considered how many people are around us every day that are masking hurt? Covering them with drugs or alcohol, or smiles and jokes, or getting lost in their work or having affairs, or practicing religion so they don't have to face the reality of their pain, insecurities, or shortcomings. The lyrics of their song is off key because of the pain and struggle inside of them, not because of who they want to be or who they are in their deepest desire."

"I believe people genuinely want better lives but suffer with knowing how to produce a better experience. When their pain and anger, discontentment or frustration surfaces and they don't have the right outlet for their pressing issues, their hurt comes out in many damaging ways. Their music, their lyrics, their song doesn't entirely reflect what they want, but it does indicate what they have become and who they are without Christ."

"So, you're saying," interjected Pal, with a semi-statement-question. "These people that do all these unusual and hurtful things are broken people? Or people that have not learned to be whole in Christ?"

"That's precisely what I believe," replied the Wise Man, "and they don't understand or trust the source completely. He is the only one who can make the repairs in their lives and heal their brokenness. Unfortunately, they continue in that same sad vein of living in silent hopelessness, frustration, anger, fear, and other facades. It's almost like they are riding an unhappy merry-go-round, unintentionally, but on a merry-go-round none the less."

"Oftentimes people are too afraid or ashamed to let someone know how they honestly feel because the exposure would be too hard to bear. So, it's easier to keep up the façade, much more comfortable than it is to deal with the change or exposure. The camouflage and the cover give them a false sense of security and a temporary escape from reality. Do you see what I mean?" the Wise Man asked Pal. "Yes, I do," Pal responded. "So again, I repeat, the music, the lyrics, the song, the habits, routines, practices, and responsibilities that speak of our lives and give credence to who we are, they're so very important," sighed the Wise Man, "that we must consider them in everything we do. I often find myself in deep reflection considering the words an old gentleman once shared with me. The thoughts he expressed to me were these ..."

Out of Touch

Racism, bigotry, prejudice, staying focused
on getting a good education, finding a safe community
to live in, getting a job with a sound healthcare plan,
finding a good church, acceptance, power ...
where do I start?
Home? School? Church?
If I start at home and mom is blind
(not devoid of sight), but blind, out of touch with reality, plus,
she's uneducated and on some type of substance
and on welfare, is that a reasonable starting point?
Dad? Who is that? I've never seen him, don't even know his name.
I developed my hand and eye coordination
fighting flies and roaches with a flyswatter.
I was watching television and I saw
some old brother speaking on racism
and playing on an even playing field.
Hello, my playing field is even, but that isn't the real problem.
I also need players with building skills and goals in mind.
Most of my neighbors are just like my mom,
and all my friends are just like me.
We are all in the dark, looking for the light.
If I start at school, it's like being at home.
There are more bodies there,
but no real caring or any positive input or influence
to pattern ourselves after.

At church, we often get our emotions stirred up
and walk out with the same picture in mind,
and it's out of focus for the same players are there.
My education, like my mother's, is limited
and she teaches me to stay in school and get an education
so, I can get a good job...which brings me back to the old brother.
I understand his plight, and I do desire the things
he's asking for:
a Job, an opportunity, a right to worship, a right to freedom
and the pursuit of happiness.
But, if I continue after them, following that old brother that
I saw on television focusing on the playing field
rather than the game,
my grandchildren and their grandchildren will be standing
outside the same stadium, trying to level the field.
To have a dream like that will make me precisely like him.
He seemed to have placed his sights on playing on the field
instead of putting his focus on being a significant player
in the game,
wherever the field may be.
I say, focus on the solutions and not the problems
that you are faced with.
The solutions are on the far side of the problems,
out of focus.
When the known is stopping you, you will never realize
the unknown;
Continue to watch the field, and you will continue to
miss the game.

"So, with that reflection, I considered letting some things go that were in me, some things that I held onto which had caused me to miss the picture, to focus on the field instead of the game. Things were keeping me from grabbing for the unknown because the known was blinding me. Although I had decent upbringing and somewhat healthy surroundings as a child, I realized I still had deep hurt and anger buried in me. Some brokenness is hard to carry, but I gave that to God and said, 'Here you hold this, your hands are stronger than mine, so you can carry this better than I can.'"

"My music, my lyrics, my song became sweeter when I let those burdens go. I still have troubles, but since my perspective has changed, my reactions to them are seen differently. Now my outlook of the field and the game have changed, and I also have a different view of people. I accept that some individuals could help make things better but don't, and I take responsibility when it's my fault when things go off track. I also recognize some selfish people choose not to change, nor do they want to see others changing for better. Nevertheless, I don't see them as the norm. Let's focus as we journey into the future," stated the Wise Man endearingly, "on being better for each other."

"Let's help one another make better choices so we can build together, not build apart. We can create a bridge that joins us, not a wall that separates us. Because life is always about choices: move, sit, walk, crawl, or run are all decisions we must make. Each of these decisions has influence in some way or another. The effects may be lasting or short-term, but we are always affected by each choice."

"It's like throwing a rock in water; the rock makes changes to the element. Whether it causes the water to ripple, splash, or create a burping sound, when it hits the water, it causes change. The change was caused by choice, not the choice of the water but by the decision of the individual who threw the rock. So often our decisions help or hurt others, and we don't even know it. Or, is it that we sometimes don't care?" He paused and looked around the room. "Nevertheless, the choices that brought us to where we are presently and the choices that made this world what it is pale considering the decisions we can make. The present decisions are paramount for a brighter tomorrow."

"I am a firm believer that every mountain is only a pile of tiny pebbles one on top of another. We can move any mountain if we join in love. We can begin growing great, long lasting relationships. We can be the beginning of the change we want to see because the road to better is calling us now. So, don't put any more pebbles on the mountain; it will just make it a bigger hill to overcome."

The Wise Man smiled and concluded his thoughts. "Actions, habits, routines, practices, and responsibilities are the keys, and what we do with these keys is dependent on what we want for our present and future generations. How willing we are to move with tenacity towards better will determine how rapidly we progress."

The Wise Man shifted his position about a half turn right as if to get a better view of everyone. He scratched his eyebrow, put his hand in his pocket, and said, "There were other lessons I learned during that time in my life. I learned we must create opportunities for ourselves occasionally, and that sometimes comparing one's self to another person can be a hindrance. I also recognized that our words and actions should be unified, and although many people may be on the field, they are not always helpers in the game."

"These were all valuable lessons along with learning how to be a significant player in the struggles of life while developing better music, lyrics, and being a living song. But, to sum it up, I must say with sincerity that although those were essential lessons, the lessons that have had the most impact in recent years are the lessons of 'never settling for less and 'staying out of the Comfort Zone.' These two concepts continue to be a present challenge for me. For example…

Why Do You Settle for Less?

The want ads read
Help needed! Upper-level manager,
master's degree in business plus four years of work experience.
Send resume to …
Here's one: Great pay, flexible hours, childcare provided.
Must have B.S. degree, call …
This one wants me to have a Ph.D.;
where does that leave me?
No slacks,
no jeans
men must wear a suit,
women must wear a dress,
they all want the best with no compromise.
Why do you want to work for them in your best suit
or dress?
They command and demand the best,
so why do you settle for less?

The Wise Man laughed and said, "In case anyone here thinks I'm trying to insult your intelligence by insinuating that you shouldn't take a good job when it's available, I'm not. That's not my point! My point is, have you ever settled for less? Have you ever done that?" He smiled briefly and asked again, "Have you settled for less instead of striving for more?"

"I believe we all have settled for less at least once or twice in our lives and it amazes me how often people do it." Exhaling slowly, he continued, "Whether it's done intentionally or not, settling for less, in my opinion, is never beneficial."

"I'm confident that everyone would like to have the best that life has to offer, but if the patience, resolve, and drive are depleted or gets lost somewhere in the shuffle and bustle of living or the hurry of having; we often lower our values and accept less than we are worth. Hmm," he exhaled thoughtfully and continued, "settling for less is a terrible practice and it has many different shapes and forms. It could hypnotize us easier than we realize. Think about it. Anyone that knows how to do better and has the means to do so but becomes lazy and indifferent has already fallen into its clutches. So, I believe everyone must be careful of feeling overfull or feeling empty. Because they are both dangerous hinderances to advancement."

"Sometimes people miss the reasoning of why challenges and struggles are in our lives. Often the most significant success is achieved in the path with the fiercest resistance and craziest obstacles. Every problem has the potential to determine how willing we are to stay in or get out of our comfort zones. Some challenges brutally force us out of the zone, while others make us dig deeper into trying to remain comfortable."

"I firmly believe contentment is beneficial. However, don't allow self-security to deaden the push needed for more growth. True contentment is being satisfied with what one has but being ready for advancement as it comes. Settling for less doesn't produce inner strength, it stops forward progression.

Which explains why so many people are stuck in bad situations. Think about the relationships that you have heard one or both partners say, 'I can't stand the sight of this person,' and yet they stay together, not because they love each other but because they are well off financially, or motivated fearfully, or are practicing some other form of settling, and none of these are productive choices."

"Please listen carefully," he said, extending his arms towards the crowd as if he was trying to hug everyone. "By no means am I promoting breakups or divorce; I'm promoting honesty. In my opinion, every relationship, especially marriage, should be one of the most stable places to be. Marriage should have integrity; If yours doesn't then maybe you're settling for less."

His arms were still extended outward as he continued, "life is not going to stop challenging us to remain in the comfort zone, and troubles certainly won't stop trying to force us to settle for less. We will need much strength and courage to move forward confidently, knowing we went in the right path. Let's be sure none of our actions are motivated by family, or peer pressure, because of fear, or to gain social acceptance. All of these are forms of settling for less."

The Wise Man looked intently from face to face and said seriously, "I strongly suggest to you, whoever you may be, not to miss the most beneficial lifetime advancements because you choose to be comfortable. Please don't take the convenient path, the shortest and easiest way, because bumps scare you."

The Wise man scratched his eyebrow reflectively. "Don't confuse the comfort zone with being comforted or content. We can find comfort during a storm and peace during a struggle. Choosing joy, peace, or strength is not the comfort zone; that is the place of being reassured. That's a good place to be!"

"Now, ask yourself this question," He paused, not a pause as if he were waiting for a response but a pause to gather his thoughts more concisely and continued with a smile saying, "What do we really gain by taking the way of settling for less and what do we ultimately lose?"

He turned slightly left and walked back to the edge of the platform. "That's the question we must ask ourselves every time we realize we're about to settle for less or recognize we already have. 'What will I eventually lose?' because settling in the comfort zone is very costly. It mars our lyrics and stains our life's music by throwing our melodies out of sync. As I said, we could compare them to high blood pressure, the silent killer who strikes without warning with disabling effects." He sighed thoughtfully, "These were hard lessons that I learned, but the benefits are now worth the trouble I caused myself now that I see things differently."

The Wise Man returned to his seat, paused for a few moments, then spoke quite rhythmically in a melodious voice. "I strive daily to make better music, sound out better lyrics, and produce better songs with my life, and I hope you feel the same about yours!"

Part VI

Mixing Colors

An elderly woman with skin the color of caramel sat watching and listening attentively to the Wise Man, her eyes followed his every movement. Other than the occasional blinking, slight moves of her head, and gestures of her hands, anyone watching her could have gotten the impression she was in a staring contest with an unseen contestant or that she was a beautiful senior mannequin with some moving parts.

The Wise Man had glanced in her direction a few times but had not seemed to take any specific notice of her. While he continued to share his thoughts about life's music, life's lyrics, and life's song, she stood up and waved her hand like an African queen in a parade, trying to get the Wise Man's attention. He finished his monologue and turned entirely in her direction. She waved once more, making sure she had his attention. "Ma'am," he said, "Is there something you would like to ask or share with us? I noticed you trying to get my attention, and I do apologize for not responding sooner, but I wanted to finish that train of thought before addressing any further comments or questions. But now the floor is yours!"

She began to speak. Her voice was aged but pleasant; it had a refined seasoned sound. And, although she spoke in soft tones, her voice held a sturdiness like antique furniture and the strength of moonshine. The deep, pure quality in her words flowed with a matter-of-fact emphasis in each noun, adjective, and verb that she used to express her thoughts.

She asked the Wise man, "Have you ever experienced a moment that begins insignificantly and becomes unforgettable? Like a single raindrop that lands on your head as you walk down the street. You glance up by force of habit not expecting anything unique or phenomenal, just looking and suddenly, in that brief interlude, grandeur happens? Have you ever experienced that?" she asked again. "Yes, I have," answered the Wise Man. "That's life," she said, "capable of starting out one way and shifting to another in any given moment."

"My name is Lodia Silverspoon. I am 83 years old. I have lived a long and fulfilling life, and I noticed listening to you that you have also lived a fascinating life." The Wise Man smiled his sentiments and nodded his head, as she continued. "I have met many different types of people and from those interactions have gathered that all people—black, white, red, yellow and whatever other colors people want to call them—basically have the same likes and dislikes, wants and desires. Each race or culture may express those wants and desires differently, but at the core, they are the same. Nevertheless, I have also come to this conclusion that nothing gets better unless people change and get better. That's what you said earlier, Sir, that nothing gets better without us getting better. So, I hope you don't mind me piggy backing on your words."

The Wise Man smiled in support again as he listened to her speak. "Furthermore," she said, "I have a saying which I've shared with my family over the years. I shared it with my sons, daughters, grandchildren, and great-grandchildren. She looked at the young woman next to her and back at the Wise Man, and back at her again. This is my great granddaughter, Chocolate, my first son's, son's child. Tell them, sweetheart, what I share with you all the time." "Big Mama, do I have to?" she said a bit reluctantly while throwing an awkward glance at her. "Yes!" she said, returning the look and laying her delicate hand on Chocolate's shoulder. "I would appreciate you sharing it with them!" Chocolate began somewhat shyly, "Big Mama always says," Lodia interjected, "Speak up my child, so they can hear you!" "Big Mama always says …"

Hope's Expectation

I try to look at people and see what God sees
when he looks at them.
I want to see without prejudice. I choose to see without bias.
I choose to see a commonness in all people; a bond beyond
race culture or ethnic group; a creed that we are created equally.
When I look at the elderly, I see a foundation and bridge.
When I look at youth, I see a magnificent sky and a flowing stream.
I choose to see people's failures as props for their most significant achievements.
I see their setbacks as springboards for the best times of their lives.
I imagine a glimmer of optimism in the eyes of a pessimist.
I believe there is a smile behind an angry man's face.
I want to see weapons of mass destruction turned into tools for mass construction.
I pray to see men as passionate about that woman in the light as he was with her in the dark.
I hope to see every desperate female find an alternative instead of having an abortion.
I pray to see every father step up to the plate of responsibility.
I pray all children are taught equality,
not inferiority or superiority.
I pray that all men will look at each other as brothers,
not as enemies, inferiors, or threats.

I pray I live to hear black people and white people not using those terms anymore.
I choose to walk a straight path on a winding street.
I choose to see possibility in impossibility's face.
I want to see other men's perspective with the right attitude.
So, I try to look at people through their eyes
so that I can see them and me differently.
I want to look at people and see what God sees
when he looks at them.
I choose to see commonness in all people;
a bond beyond race, culture, or ethnic group,
a creed that we are one.
I choose to see hope's expectations.

"That's what she says she chooses, and she tells us that wisdom is like seven pillars that hold the building up and won't let it fall. Big Mama always says that godly wisdom is a fountain of fresh water which we should drink from daily. She reminds us that if we use God's wisdom in our ways and actions, things will go well. She says, His wisdom will refresh our souls and help us through the day because we never know what the day will bring."

"She says wisdom is acquired from experiences good or bad, but the bad ones seem to stick with us the longest and we should always be grateful. Honesty and trust are the roots of the tree of peace.'"

Chocolate somewhat rolled her eyes, but not in the direction of her great-grandmother. "She tells me every day to be careful how I view other people because I am not exempt from falling or making some life-changing mistake. Everyone is always one step away from up or down, falling or rising, she continuously says. She also reminds me daily," Chocolate paused briefly, then continued. "She reminds me to trust God and do good and know for sure that …"

O.W.L.

Our
wisdom
lingers …
when we have grown
with those we have taught.
When we have given out
and taken in, in right portions
and proportions equally.
When we have shared
and not held back,
in spite of distractions
or factions,
or oppositions,
from lessor or higher powers,
endeavoring to see improvements
in the present generation,
and generations that follow.
Our
wisdom
lingers!

"Hope's expectations and enduring wisdom, that's what my Big Mama always says is important for living our best lives." Chocolate looked at her great-grandmother with eyes of endearment and relief that she wouldn't be required to say anything else. Lodia's request had been fulfilled. Chocolate sat down, but Lodia remained standing.

"Those are the words I share and have shared for quite a while," said Lodia. "Life has shown me by experience what makes men act as they do when they don't act with Godly wisdom!" She looked at the Wise Man intently, then shifted her aged frame towards those standing around her and said, "I have one last thing I would like to share." Turning slowly towards the Wise Man again, she said very politely, "Sir, indulge me just for a few more moments, and I promise to get out of the way!" The Wise Man smiled and said, "Please continue, I've enjoyed every word that's been shared thus far, and I am very confident your next thoughts shall be just as profound and helpful as what you had your great-granddaughter share for you." "Thank you," Lodia said, smiling graciously and began sharing her views.

Just One Taste

In the garden by the exquisite tree,
man lost his innocence,
forfeiting the image of God to become like gods.
Just one taste of the forbidden.
Just one taste of the unknown.
Just one taste from the tree
of the knowledge of good and evil.
They did not know it was a rotten tree,
corrupted with pride in its roots,
and selfishness its steely trunk.
Because it was so pleasant to look upon,
and it was so desirous to look at,
beauty is guile's most alluring attraction,
beauty is deception's most pleasant tool.
Murder and betrayal were in every branch,
corruption and woe its tasty fruit.
In its shade, there was a deceptive comfort,
a bizarre shadow casting puzzling light,
sly and blinding.
Just one taste of the forbidden, only one taste of the unknown,
and the seed of the tree was planted
in humanity's soul
to be passed onto every generation.
How could they know its tasty fruit
was for the destruction of men and nations?
How could they know its fruit

would corrupt the heart of man
and pierce the heart of God?
They did not know that all humanity
would be yoked together by one decision.
They did not know the high price of their adventure.
They were unaware of the tragedy it would produce.
They didn't know they had given death a license
to reap in season everything born on earth.
They did not know they had lost their real life.
All they knew ...
was that they were naked and ashamed.

Lodia didn't say another word. She sat down as she had promised. Chocolate handed her a handkerchief to wipe the perspiration from her face. For a few eternal moments, the Wise Man didn't say anything either. The room was vibrating yet silent; alive with the energy of the words just shared, quiet in the moment of reflection.

"Those words took me back to my childhood," said the Wise Man. "My mother used to share that story with me. The story of the fall of humanity in the Garden of Eden. That's a profound and thought-provoking lesson on bad choices. Choices that set the course of humanity in motion and filled man with many distractions. That choice gave humanity ideas that it believes are always grand and beneficial. Although some concepts may very well be impressive and quite ingenious and helpful, not all notions are rooted in the graces that promote good will for all men."

"I am certain two of the most essential tools humanity possesses are belief and knowledge, but both become futile when not used, and very dangerous when misused. So, I keep in mind the wisdom of God in a man will guide him correctly, but man's knowledge alone is limited at best."

The Wise Man adjusted his collar, wiped his mouth, and continued. "I believe man's greatest dilemma is finding the right path to follow. I also believe God gives us a perfect path to follow but allows us to choose for ourselves if we want to follow it or not. Since there truly is no road that leads nowhere, every man's challenge is just like in the garden: obedience to God's path or following our own."

"Listen," said the Wise Man very pointedly, "we choose the road, but we cannot choose the consequences that happen on that route, nor can we choose the outcome. The benefits and the struggles are on the path we choose whether it's God's path or our own. And everything we do in this entire life is under the watchful eye of God, both good and evil. People motivated or blinded by their overwhelming desires seldom consider the overall consequences of their actions and the lasting effect it will have on them and others. Looking through the eyes of greed or lust, or through the eyes of increase and expansion for their cause makes the end justify the means. And, makes it much easier for them to make decisions in that vein of thought."

"It may appear that I am revisiting a subject already discussed when I spoke of the extra mile. However, bear with me for a little longer while I share these thoughts with you. I often contemplate man's motives." He paused and readjusted his collar. "Let's discuss man's intentions for doing the things he does and his drive to achieve at all cost. We should question our real motivation when we act, or when we do the things, we consider to be progressive or beneficial for the future of us and others. We should genuinely search ourselves and ask, 'Are my motives self-serving, self-gratifying, or selfish? Or, am I genuinely considering others and how it will pan out for them and me?'"

"People are basically centered around how things will best serve them," the Wise Man said, shaking his head slowly. "Even cultural Christianity has followed that move, however, from the pope to the president to the poop-scooper, everyone should think of how their actions affect others and keep that in mind before they speak or act." "That would help," said Pal. Lodia nodded her head as well as others with the same thoughts.

"Especially in this presumably Christian nation," stated the Wise Man thoughtfully. "We know there are always at least two sides to everything except God's truth. God's truth is the only thing absolute. Everything else has the possibility of having flaws." He paused reflectively, looking upward, then lowered his head slowly and segued into another avenue. "I don't knock scientific discovery, nor am I against scientific research; however, I do ask myself the question of how many people are being replaced by robots or other machinery that has made the process of production faster. I believe we should be progressive because society is moving. Nevertheless, I also think we must be cautious in our progression because those very things that we trust can cause us the most problems."

"By nature, man," said the Wise Man as he motioned towards the ceiling, "is always reaching and grabbing outward as he attempts to hold onto something which can hold him and at the same time, he's trying to take hold of something he can possess. From birth, he reaches out because he wants to achieve and wants security. He also wants satisfaction and is motivated to discover things within and beyond his reach to satisfy the desire pushing him."

"That's right," Chocolate interjected, as others nodded in agreement. "My mother said when I was a child, I would not let her finger go! I was continually grabbing for things. I was in discovery mode all the time. And she would have a difficult time prying anything out of my hand. I wanted to know as much as I could about as many things as possible. I wanted to be well rounded and I am still reaching!"

The Wise Man marched on with his thoughts. "So, every person has deeply rooted in them a push by reflex and desire to have and hold what they think is valuable, interesting, or necessary.

There's also a thrust in people which makes them attempt to reach beyond this momentary desire."

"It is embedded in the deepest desire of mankind," reflected the Wise Man verbally, "a longing for the tree that sustains life.

Because man wants to live, and he wants to last in the memories of others. So, everyone is attempting to grab or build something that will outlast this temporal existence."

"Therefore, the glory of being recognized as the inventor, or the founder, or the progenitor of this or that, or just having a memorable name, often moves people with force more potent than winds blowing 120 mph. Sadly, too often, the things people do and the things people build become the wings they believe will carry them to a higher realm of existence. Because in the human heart is that longing to have something that lasts. I repeat," said the Wise Man pointedly, "Civilization's efforts and humanities building consistently display the fact of people wanting life to last past this temporary reality."

"However, since man knows he will pass on, he builds monuments to himself, hoping his name will endure in the memoirs of humanity." The Wise Man snickered in a saddened way and continued the monologue. "It's as if people are always grabbing for bigger, better, faster, almost like being in 'Six Million Dollar Man' mode continuously. In man's quest to achieve the most phenomenal, most fantastic, most dynamic something ever accomplished, or merely to make his mark, he often goes off track from the single road that God has set before him. A humble path of obedience that yields an enormous increase."

"Consider this," said the Wise Man reflectively. "The life that man chooses for himself or the wings that men make for themselves with finite wisdom is futile when viewed in infinite light. Believe me, his human efforts will never fly him as high, guide him as straight, nor function for him as well as the wings that God graciously wants to give him to fly him along the path designed for him. So, either greed's desire births egotistical ambitions or is its selfish ambitions that birth greed's desire? Or pure human ambition births uncontrolled desires, which then pushes humanity to grab for everything they want for themselves, instead of what God wants for them. I'm not exactly sure how to word it, but anyway we look at it, it's a path and wings that will inevitably lead to a metal door and an iron ceiling. Because nothing on this earth is eternal but the soul of a human, and that's all we take with us beyond this temporal existence. That's why I said we must be mindful of what our intentions are in the things we build and the things we do. Because faulty desires and misguided intentions and life separated from the Lord will take people down a slippery path, as man did in that tree." The Wise Man looked around, waiting for comments or responses.

Sgt. Robin Sparrow moved forward through the crowd like a man on a mission. An aura of confidence covered him like a garment. Everything about him said military structure: his movements, his hand gestures, his look all said soldier prepared for battle. His face was like flint; his eyes entirely focused on the next move he would make to get closer to the stage where the Wise Man stood expressing his thoughts.

Somewhere near the stage, a small voice spoke out. It belonged to a young girl; she couldn't have been more than twelve years old. "Sir, Sir," she said in her preteen voice, "Why is the world so crazy? Why do people do mean things? Couldn't we just fix the problem? There has to be a way to fix it…" The girl's voice trailed off as she realized everyone's eyes were fixed on her. She ducked down slightly, but the Wise Man told her to stand up as he addressed her questions.

"What would you like to see fixed?" asked the Wise Man. "The world! I mean the people! I mean everybody!" she said, unsure of how to express her feelings. "Well, that's a very tall order," replied the Wise Man, "but not impossible. Not impossible for the Lord but a man with his strength alone, with his faulty wings, following the path he's made for himself, never!"

"We don't have the power or the wisdom to do it, but if we would all surrender and follow the simple plan of God, things would line themselves up. Do you understand what I mean? he asked her. "I think so," she replied, though uncertainly. He smiled and continued. "The cruelty, the hurt, the hate, the thought of white entitlement would all be resolved if people would love each other and Mary's baby born in a manger."

She smiled and asked, "Are you talking about little baby Jesus?" "Yes," the Wise Man responded. "Oh, yes!" she giggled sheepishly. "I love him, and someday I'm gonna meet him! But I don't think he's a baby anymore!" "No, he's not," said the Wise Man. "He's fully grown and sitting right next to his father." "Do you love him?" she asked the Wise Man. "Yes, I do, and very much." She and the Wise Man smiled at each other a few more lingering moments and just before he could speak again ...

Sgt. Robin Sparrow said, "Excuse me, Sir," introduced himself and began speaking with the passion and authority of a man used to power. "Humanity must be directed in the right path, and our nation must also be as well. I remember my grandmother telling me to treat everyone with kindness no matter who they were.

She always reminded me that it would be rewarded. She told me to always go the extra mile and trust God in everything." He glanced in the direction of Lodia and Chocolate, and then at the young girl. "And I believed her then. But I am a man now, and I see the cruelties of this world and the crazies that live in it.

I've been far and wide fighting for our freedoms and risking my life to protect our liberties. I've watched mad men do some of the cruelest things possible, and I tried to believe there was some good in everyone, but my experiences have made me question many things. You know, sometimes I can't help but question some things that I've learned."

"Why must I turn the other cheek? Why do I have to give kindness and never retaliate with malice? Why do I have to love those who don't love me? Where is the fairness? Where is justice when dictators overthrow regimes to implement their wills or when children are thrown into war due to the leader's insanity? Truly, it doesn't make sense to me when our own country does many sketchy and questionable things that raise my eyebrows and make me think about what we really mean when we say, "in God we trust!"

"So, yes, you are right. Mr. Wise-man, Sir, we do need help, but do you think we can get it from a baby supposedly born in a manger who was later said to be nailed to a cross and then miraculously rose from death? Doesn't that seem a bit farfetched? I mean those stories are suitable for children and those who are insecure or need something to hope for but for us? Come on, Sir?"

The young girl looked at the Wise man and at Sgt. Sparrow, who was staring at the Wise man with an expression that said, "Do you really believe the story of Jesus?"

"It's obvious," said the Wise Man with a sentiment in his voice, "that you allowed time and life to change your view. I come to this conclusion because you said you believed your grandmother when she shared her thoughts with you." "I was a child," Sgt. Sparrow interjected, "unwise to the reality of the real dirt of the world." "I understand," said the Wise Man, "but the fact remains you believed her. From that reality, I can gather that somewhere you either got the thought that your grandmother lied to you or she was only telling you those stories about Jesus to cripple and handicap you. Or, just for you to have a toy to play with within your mind while you grew up."

"Surely every grandmother is seeking a way to hold their grandchildren back, or as hostages and dependent on them. Or, maybe they are just trying to protect them from all the cruelties of the world. So, they make up imaginative stories to make them feel better for the moment, knowing that sooner or later, the brick of truth will hit them in the face and abruptly wake them up."

"Very funny, Sir," responded Sgt. Sparrow. "But no, not at all, my grandmother was a very straightforward woman, she meant what she said. She didn't play games with words or semantics.

My grandmother and father are the reasons I chose military service. So, no I'm not saying she deliberately lied, but I am saying maybe she just used that to keep me in line, or as a scare tactic or something like that."

"That's an interesting viewpoint," said the Wise Man, "and I am sure there are others who join in that view that feel they are too intelligent to believe something so simple as faith in a man they cannot see. But they believe air exists every day, but they cannot see it. There is dust in it! Things are moved by it! But, see it? Air? Nah! And, I am not trying to insult your intelligence!"

"What you're trying to tell me," Sgt. Sparrow replied, "is that you genuinely believe that Jesus existed and walked on this earth? And that he is the answer to men's problems?" "Yep, that's correct," said the Wise Man. Sgt. Sparrow chuckled a bit sarcastically and said, "No offense to you, Sir, my dad or my grandmother, but it seems just a bit surreal! Why would any man do such a thing?"

"Because of love and understanding, the necessity of it," replied the Wise Man.

"You're a soldier, aren't you?" said the Wise Man rhetorically. "Yes! We've established that already," responded Sgt. Sparrow, a bit edgy. The Wise Man continued, "Okay, good, I'll use this as an example! You go everywhere you're sent and fight to defend freedoms for that country and ours. However, you didn't have anything to do with the conflict, but because you understand the necessity of freedom and the value of it, you risk your life continuously. In your heart, I would dare to say is your family and the other families whose lives you seek to protect. In your mind, is the thought of liberty. So, with that awareness and the orders from the general, you go to battle, conscious of death all around you, right? You have decided that if it is necessary that you die for the freedom of others, so be it."

"That's the picture of Jesus; he went to battle that we could be free. He gave his life so that we could have life. His father is the general that gave the orders, and he is the soldier that freely died for all mankind." "Well, I never thought of it like that," said Sgt. Sparrow. The Wise Man smiled and said, "Let me share with you and everyone here what your grandmother and dad may or may not have shared in this way."

Golgotha

Golgotha
was not a pretty place.
No soft leather or lace,
no silk sheets on Sealy Posturepedic,
and beyond just therapeutic,
it delivered such eternal grace
from that battered face and thorn-bruised brow
that somehow, miraculously
the whole world could be made free.
That light from eternity,
heaven's beam that shined brightly
first uttered, "forgive them"
Those words were for me
and every soul
that would bow before his grace,
and put down their proud and lofty sinfulness
to accept the eternal bliss
from him, who betrayed by a kiss
did hang in the sorrow and joy of the day
on the rugged unkind cross, obediently
to pay the price for humanity's blackened ways.
Those nails which held those precious feet and hands;
that spear which in his side was thrust
were harsh and they were fierce demands
from a father who loves all humanity
but hates sin much more.

So that release of blood and water,
and that final glorious holler
"It is finished," still rings through the generations
and lands on those who dare to trust
in him that bore and wore
the ugliness of Golgotha.

The Wise Man looked very sincerely at Sgt. Sparrow and said, "Your grandmother wasn't telling you some charming bedtime story. Nor was she giving you the hoax of some traditional fairy tale which present a pseudo-reality to make us feel good and help merchants make money. She wasn't giving you a lioness blanket or a crutch for the weak and helpless, something to stick hope in when you have nothing else—no, not at all. Your grandmother and dad were giving you what they knew in their heart would be the best guide and compass ever. They were giving you an anchor to hold you steady, a pillar to lean on guaranteed to hold you up, and a pillow to lay your head on when you need rest."

The Wise Man went further, "If this man Jesus is unreal, untrue and so unbelievable, why is time centered around him? We say A.D. and B.C. Why not count time by Hannibal, Caesar, or Alexander the Great? Or any of the other great men in history? Why count it by Jesus? What makes him so unique? Did someone draw straws out of a hat, and he got the luck of the draw? If Jesus is not who the Bible says he is, why would so many believers throughout the generations base their entire lives on a non-existent character? No one would do that!"

"Christians have faced constant persecution and trouble for their beliefs; they have been treated as badly as the nation of Israel.

Jesus is Jewish. So, if He is not who he says he is, if He is not the Son of the living God, why does he cause so much controversy? And, if people can gravitate to a rabbit laying eggs, and a jolly man with flying reindeer, why is it so hard to believe in Jesus as a savior?"

"Is it that those other things do not require an allegiance, and Jesus does? Jesus requires a total commitment, and they don't. Is it that Jesus is the only one who can truly say he was resurrected, is that the issue? Maybe the biggest problem is that we have convinced ourselves that we are pretty good and there is nothing wrong with us. We believe that admitting that there is an inherent problem in all of humanity would be too risky because then every individual would have to take a closer look at themselves and say, 'I need help,' which brings me back to my initial thought," said the Wise Man jovially. "Jesus does offer all humanity help, but because people have an 'I can-fix-this-one- myself-mentality,' the most excellent rescue ever provided is often turned down."

"Hold up! Stop the train!" interjected a man standing just a few feet away from Sgt. Sparrow and slightly behind Lodia. "What you're saying is we all have a problem that we don't want to face, and Jesus is the only one who can fix it." "I completely agree with Sgt. Sparrow," he stated, looking in his direction. "Something is very wrong in this world, but I don't think Jesus is the cure all!

The Wise Man was standing with his arms crossed over his chest and one hand on his chin, listening intently to the man's comments. "Let me make this as clear as possible," said the Wise Man, as his eyes scanned the room. "Many decent people in the world do great humanitarian things. These people have good morals; they're helpful and do good deeds. They're the ones who assist their neighbors any way they can. They're friendly and polite and are often considered pillars in their community.

Some of these same people work on committees to make cities better, assist young boys and girls grow into maturity, and even help old people cross the street."

The Wise Man unfolded his arms and continued. "These are decent people who possess all the things we call favorable, and their good deeds are commendable. However, none of these great things can change the inherent problem in people. Sin! Very simple, very concise. Sin! Sin is in every person born in this world, and that's the problem. And because it's in all of humanity, every individual needs a covering of it, a cleansing from it, and the power to overcome it. That's what Jesus represents: the covering, the cleansing and the power. Disavowing this truth causes the initial problem and the conflict because people do not want to see themselves as sinners. We will see and accept ourselves as everything but that. And that's what everyone is without Jesus, a sinner, lost and condemned."

"Isn't this the same thing you told us earlier?" asked a lady suggestively. "No, not precisely," replied the Wise Man, "but it is along the same lines. Previously I said God loves everyone; now I'm telling you how he expressed that love and why." The Wiseman's eyes were as shiny as diamonds as he expressed his thoughts.

Calvary

God's champion was hanging on the cross, facing death to
pay the cost of all mankind which was lost
through Adam's disobedience.
Darkness held the land tightly, the sun refused to shine
brightly, between two crooks being punished justly,
hung divine innocence.
Obediently as the sacrifice,
the Son of God, the man called Christ
would give His life to pay the price that no one else could pay.
His blood was for the atonement
of sin which had brought God's judgment
on mankind, so He was sent to face that terrible day.
He hung there suffering long, though weak in His flesh,
His spirit was strong; He brought back man where he belonged,
where His last breath was relinquished.
His voice went out in sweet forgiveness,
His voice cried out in bitter anguish.
"Victoriously," He said, "It is finished!" then He released His
spirit proving no man took His life, that He laid it down
a sacrifice
which was the father's chosen price
to satisfy His just requirement.
Now all people in every generation
from all kindred, tongues or nations
can come to the fount of salvation
and be covered by the blood's atonement.

Yes, that precious lamb called Christ, to please the father gave His life; to remove our sins, He paid the price so
that all men could be free. That blood through the generations, that blood sprinkled on the nations,
that blood which brings salvation is extended to you and me.

The Wise Man looked around and continued, "But the most challenging and simple choice anyone will ever make is to believe in the Son of God, the Son of man who says eternity is in his hands and all people must come through him to get the best life now and a blessed eternity."

"I say it's easy because it's just a matter of saying 'I want the help'; yet difficult because man's highest hurdle is himself. The other problem that makes it hard to grab is, if people accept that they are sinners not by choice but by birth, they will have to face the fact that cleansing is necessary. So, it's more convenient to hold onto the belief of 'I'm ok' 'I'm a good person,' than to grab hold of what God says is available for humanity's help. Also, I believe the problem gets larger wings," said the Wise Man still smiling, "because people want eternity, but they want it their way. Therefore, they manufacture many ways to get eternity's bliss. Somewhat like building a tower of Babel which will ultimately end in confusion. One of the saddest facts in life is that help is available, but it's rejected daily because it's just too hard to accept; we are sinners by birth, but we continue sinning by choice."

"I also find that interesting," interjected Lodia. The man near Lodia and Sgt. Sparrow who had said 'hold the train' had his arms crossed in a defiant stance but didn't say anything. He just stared at the Wise Man sullenly. The Wise Man looked his way and continued. "Although people want to live forever, and no one wants to die, they still refuse someone who is offering help when Jesus says, 'this is the only way to get it.' He declares, 'I am the way, the truth, and the life, and no man comes to the Father but by me.' But, instead of taking the simple offer, they conjure many self-made methods and celebrate the idols they have made. Nevertheless, Christ truly paid it all while hanging on the cross; whatever the 'it is,' that holds any person hostage, it's connected to the sin-nature in man, and Christ's sacrifice can free them from it. But it's up to the individual to surrender to his offer."

"If humanity continues to paddle in the big cesspool of sinfulness attempting to fix themselves with ingenuity, human resource, and scientific advancements, mankind will continue to degenerate. Because Christ is the answer for every dilemma, for any injustices, for all corruption, and for removing the idols that we have made. The doubt that grabs our hearts, minds, and souls can be replaced with peace through him. He's the only answer for sin!"

Sgt. Sparrow turned and looked at the man who was standing so defiantly behind Lodia. Then, he turned and looked at the young girl next to him with a smile. Finally, he turned towards the Wise Man and said, "Thank you, I have much to consider, and I appreciate how you explained this today. I'll be leaving soon to go on another assignment, but I will not forget what you have said." Sgt. Robin Sparrow saluted the Wise Man; the Wise Man returned the salute, and as they gazed at each other, there was a certain aura that said all would be well.

The Wise Man watched him weaving towards the exit but was brought back to the moment by a middle-aged lady who somewhat startled him. "Your comments deeply moved me; I have the same conviction!" "That's great," said the Wise Man smiling. She continued, "But many don't share our views, and no one has the power to change their perspective but them. Just like the ant which climbed that tree continuously and struggled seeing anything different; their opinion is theirs to have and share with anyone that will listen, just as you are sharing yours today."

"There was also a time I pondered what or who could fix these issues in our society. I was exactly like that young girl." She nodded in the youth's direction. "I also said, 'Can't we just fix it?'" Then, looking at the defiant man, she said, "I was also like you, Sir, but one day, after careful consideration I realized Jesus is the only answer. He's the only one-shoe-fits-all available to man." She returned her attention to the Wise Man and said, "I would like to share the thoughts I had with everyone if it's okay with you?" "Please, be my guest," said the Wise Man politely. She smiled slightly and said, "I thought about …"

Man's Question. God's Statement.

What if …
Man, in his quest
to establish himself
to advance himself
to prove himself
as an independent entity,
as inevitably proven man without Christ
lives in organized chaos,
instability and speculation
in its highest form of sophistication.

She looked around the room at the gatherers and expressed another thought.

Memories

While strolling through the hallways of the memories of my mind, I dusted off the pictures of the thoughts I left behind. Some were in dark shadows; they could not have been too kind, for the hands that reached out to me, I left them all behind. Some were in the meadows, where the sun did brightly shine, some were along the babbling brooks, where lilies all were lined. Some were above the mountaintops, where my heart would slowly climb. Some were near the ocean shore, where the waves would often roar. Some were among the pillory clouds, where the seagulls did freely soar.

I lingered near the door of a dream I laid aside
while the sands of yesterday's mistakes
eroded like the ebbing of the tide. I counted all the steps down the stairwell of my soul and strolled through the pathway of tranquility to the park in my mind. I sat on the bench of brotherhood, but there I sat alone pondering ways to free the world of hate, greed, and strife. But I could not come up with any solution to save my life. Suddenly upon the wings of reality, it occurred to me that in another life and time, this would have to be
suddenly upon the wings of reality, it occurred to me
that in another life and time, this would have to be!

She finished speaking and looked directly into the Wise Man's eyes. The gatherers were all looking at the Wise Man and his reaction. "Hmm…" said the Wise Man, his eyebrows shifting downward in contemplation. "Yes, I see your point, we have the desire for accord on earth even when it's not always the case; yet in eternity," the Wise Man said smiling, "there will be perpetual peace, love, and brotherhood; and the Lord is the one that will bring that harmony."

The Wise Man looked at everyone very sincerely while stating, "Peace is the offspring of love, as corruption is the offspring of hate. Harmony is the progeny of unity, as discord is the offspring of hostility, and sadly, there will never be agreement among all people until humanity surrenders to God and people are freed from sin. Therefore, if we would live our lives considering eternity, I believe it would give people a different perspective."

"Since we leave a mark on all things here and we carry a mark with us, what will the legacy be that we leave behind and what will the identification be that we take with us?" He rubbed his chin reflectively and continued his thought. 'If it isn't fatal, it isn't final' that's what my buddy said, and I agree. Therefore, anyone living has an opportunity to grab for new horizons and change the way they're thinking by grabbing the giver of life.

Knowing Christ helps us journey through this life with a promise of victory no matter how bad our present state may be. The moment anyone decides to take His offer is the moment that begins the process of overcoming the most challenging areas of settling for less. It's amazing!"

The Wise Man smiled, cleared his throat with a cough and continued his reflections. "I often think about life beyond this life. I seriously think about eternity," he smiled gently and continued speaking.

In Light of Eternity

Eternity,
Oh, endless eternity,
there is much to learn from you
for you are not restricted
to finite space, time, or view
and you shall in your own time
bring all things in your presence
and there shall not be one thing
that does not experience your essence.
You are not like humans with flaws and limitations
that stymy your infinite station.
You see the crude travelers we are
with your clear vision.
We travel from day to day
beneath auspicious or ominous skies,
Onward journeying through the temporary
until we look you in the eyes.
And in displaying your wisdom,
you allow the temporary to exist
in the presence of forever that humanity
might yearn for what's endless
for short it is our stay here.
It is a vapor less than a gasp
and we will vanish like mist,
floating mystically from wet grass.
Never to return to this side of destiny.

No, we shall move forward to eternity,
Oh, endless eternity
that always says beyond,
not yesterday.

The Wise Man looked straight ahead as if he was looking into an unseen realm and continued. "It's interesting, in a sad way, that eternity doesn't seem to hold humanity's attention or have the attractiveness that the temporary does."

Chocolate interjected her thoughts. "Maybe it's because temporary things appeal to people's senses: taste, touch, hear, smell, see and all that accommodates the momentary experience."

"That's correct," responded the Wise Man, "however, eternity is much more beautiful, much more profound. It is connected to the invisible realm of hope, which is seen by faith. Therefore, the invisible realm of eternity is far more valuable than anything we can see now with physical eyes."

"It is true what was written by the prophet Isaiah, then quoted by the apostle Paul, 'Eye hath not seen, nor ear heard, neither hath entered into the heart of man, the things which God hath prepared for them that love him. But, God hath revealed them unto us by His Spirit; for the Spirit searcheth all things, yea, the deep things of God (KJV).' So, shifting our eyes from our temporal existence to our eternal existence, while staying focused on the tasks at hand is never easy. Simply because it requires mankind to relinquish that which people rely on most, 'sight belief.' Eternity operates on the principle of 'faith-belief!' Therefore, the choice is believing what God says eternity holds for the faithful or groping around in the darkness, living out this temporal experience with eyes wide open. Yet, blinded to the reality of the more significant things beyond this human experience; that the Lord only gives to those who trust him by faith."

"This is the big picture in a small package—living each day in the thought of eternity or living each day without giving it much thought. Remember Jesus said, 'Layup treasures for yourselves in heaven where the moth and the rust won't eat it up' (KJV)."

He smiled and continued, "So, I think about eternity often and live in reflection of this thought found in Hebrews chapter eleven, 'Now faith is the substance of things hoped for, the evidence of things not seen. For by it, the elders obtained a good report (KJV).' Therefore, the only way to receive the benefits of eternity are to look with the eyes of faith ... and faith must be connected to the unchanging word of the Lord. When one looks at the future through that lens, their spirit soars like an eagle. Because they realize the treasure it holds for Christians, they await the future promises and the Father who made them. The God who will not fail, the God who cannot lie, will welcome his children home. Are you prepared to meet Him in eternity?"

Part VII

Final Touches

"That was quite refreshing," said the Wise Man jovially as he entered back into the building alongside a few of the guest. "It's a lovely afternoon. I mean, giving up such a beautiful day to spend time with me is very special and I shall place it among my memoirs with much appreciated gratitude."

"We didn't want to miss this opportunity to spend time with you," the guest replied in harmony. "That's very considerate," responded the Wise Man, "and those insights you shared, I'll cherish them as keepsakes." He returned to his seat, cleared his throat with a sip of water and began sharing again.

"While outside chatting with a few of you, the thought crossed my mind of how amazing this world is. How it continually revives and renews itself; how it survives natural disasters. These things seem to destroy nature but never entirely because God has placed in the earthly realm what it takes for it to survive. Nature shows us the spirit needed to bounce back because God has also placed in us the same thing he put in nature, the ability to keep growing and moving forward."

"Every day gives us a new chance and opportunity to grow and become better in view of eternity. Just as nature repeatedly shouts, 'This day is a new beginning,' and then displays this with an unwavering persistence that todays a day to grab for what's beyond with all the enthusiasm one can muster. Consider this. No matter how many times you mow the lawn it will grow back, and no matter how bad the elemental conditions, the tree remains faithful with its branches lifted in thankfulness even when its stripped of its leaves."

"Let us be as persistent as grass and as faithful as a tree as we live from day to day. We must have that same attitude. Let me challenge and encourage you," said the Wise Man grinning joyfully.

Climb On

New beginnings can be compared to
freehand mountain climbing,
a task of endurance and patience
which challenges the strength
within ourselves to confront
a world waiting to be experienced
full of wonderful God-given opportunities.
Climb on,
continuing to progress
one hand, one foot, completely balanced
synchronized movement,
wisely looking ahead,
not behind nor downward too often;
below lies the old not forgotten,
just used as a motivating factor
to continue moving forward,
realizing with every forward movement that
new horizons will be nearer and
the old ones further away.

"I repeat," he said grinning while wagging his finger confidently back and forth like the tail of a dog, "If it isn't fatal, it isn't final. All we need is the desire, the motivation, and the faith to push past what attempts to hold us up and hold us back. Repetitive practice of anything makes it a habit hard to break, but anything can be changed. Life is continuously giving us another chance, and although we can ease into the comfort zone, it's possible to overcome any obstacle. But, it's always about a choice. Not even the slightest movement forward can be performed without a decision."

The Wise Man gestured with his finger again and pointedly stated, "Don't use the rearview mirror to go forward; it takes up too much time and energy. Stay focused on the present moment, yesterday's mistakes are not meant to be carried today. So, don't take them with you as you start to climb the mountain or run the hurdles. Remember freehand climbers and hurdlers don't wear backpacks. Perhaps you will think about this whenever you feel stuck or feel like you're facing a wall." He then smiled broadly and shared these words of encouragement.

Inner Strength

A wall can be caused to fall
even if it's big or small,
and it doesn't matter how tall
it may appear to be,
For in the end,
it will depend
not on the wall my friend,
but on the determination
that lives in you or me.

"Therefore, encourage yourself; the possibility to succeed is in you and if you are willing to try, I am certain you can make it. My only suggestion is that, as you move forward to not let the walls of doubt be your stop sign. Let the walls challenge you to climb them, go around them, speak to them, or knock them down. But never let walls of discouragement be your camping grounds. Use them as the motivation to excel to greater heights."

"Many people wish for improvement, but they want that improvement to come and grab them, pick them up, and carry them on a floating carpet. Although a floating carpet is highly unlikely, miracles are possible. However, even miracles require that you put in the effort of accepting them. It's the same with new opportunities; they are presented all the time, but if we do not see them, believe them, and move,

I guarantee we will not accomplish anything in that new opportunity." He chuckled, as his eyes beamed humorously, "That's the one thing I can assure you of, no matter how many times new opportunities come to our door, they will not walk for us or work for us. We must do the walking and working ourselves!"

His brow wrinkled slightly as he spoke. "Never feel inadequate, even if you are not the one with the degree, your skillset may make the difference, so don't count yourself out. Am I downplaying education? Not at all! Pursue all the academics your mind can handle. Nevertheless, if you don't have a college education, it doesn't mean you're inadequate or less important than someone who does. Do you realize how many people with degrees in America are jobless? While many others with degrees aren't working in their field of study! Let me be very honest with you," the Wise Man said off-handedly, "I do not have a degree, but that never held me back. Education is a powerful tool that I view aptly, but I can never allow any lack of academics to define me, nor should you let it define you. You may have a God given talent that causes you to outshine everyone. And, if you don't have that, then there are skills and trades you can learn. Whatever your desires and interest are, do all you can to grow in them because it may be your highest potential for success."

Special Gift

You have a gift!
Unique as a rock or a diamond.
Refined or unrefined, it's in you,
an ability that sets you apart
from every individual among the millions.
Perhaps your gift is the tool to build empires
or treehouses in back yards.
It could be designed to wipe away one tear
and change a life forever.
It could be designed to bring stability in chaos.
It could be the vision the next generation climbs on
or the bedrock that this generation stands on.
What if your gift is the sails the wind needs
to push the nation's growth or to confront local injustices,
or just to protect a child in your neighborhood?
Wouldn't you want to use that gift?
Wouldn't you want to discover its potential
and use it to destroy a wall then build a bridge?
Wouldn't you want to use it for every possible good and
then say to God that gave it to you,
this is what I did with your gift.
Or, do you want the gift to lie dormant?
Buried inside you like unmined salt
that never added to the world it's seasoning.

"Think about it," said the Wise Man. "What if your special gift is lying dormant in you? Is that what we want? A great gift lying dormant, unused and wasting away?"

The Wise Man smirked and leaned forward like he was about to share a secret, then continued speaking. "And to those here that have been working at a job for a long time, but want to try something new, remember not to settle for less. It could be that new field of interest is what you are designed to do. It could possibly fulfill some of the longing in you that's been missing at your present job. And, even if the change you need has nothing to do with a job, the power to accomplish greater is inside of you. Therefore, as opportunities present themselves, be watchful not to miss them. Because your life's purpose may be connected to that opportunity." Pausing just slightly to shift position and scratch his forehead, he continued his thoughts.

The Wise Man looked very thoughtful and reflective, "So as I was saying, there are always new opportunities being presented

and often the opportunity that presents itself is presented to bring out the power of your gift. Your powerful ability."

The Wise Man grinned and was about to continue when he was interrupted. "Are you saying that we all have special powers or something like that?" asked the young man with the orange neon t-shirt, humorously. The Wise Man responded, "Not so much like special powers in the sense of being Superman, able to fly and look through buildings and things. Nah, that's not my point. We all know that's not humanly possible!"

The young man grinned at the Wise Man's reply. "What I am saying is, we all have a specific assignment in this life, and God has given everyone a special gift, a unique ability, and a particular purpose. That ability can bring them before great men.

In other words, each of us has a gift like no one else on earth.

And, no one will be able to use it as well as the one who possesses it can. Not a superpower, but a unique ability."

"For example: Samson was strong, Solomon was wise, Joan of Arc was brave, Einstein was a mathematical genius, George Washington Carver was a brilliant scientist, just to name a few.

I could have called up others as examples, but I chose these to show their diversity and the fact that it doesn't matter where you are from, what your conditions are, your race or your gender, nor does it matter the time frame in which you exist. The fact is you have a gift which is designed for your use and the benefit of humanity."

"Nothing was just haphazardly placed on earth. All species, even fungi has a specific purpose. Imagine how important the most intelligent creation is. Man is the highest representative of God. It would be insane for the Creator to make anything which would represent himself and not give it at least one standout quality and ability. Surely, we can all agree on that point!" The Wise Man sighed and continued to speak.

Light

Lord, remind us there is your light in us;
the beautiful light of ability.
Then, we will allow ourselves
to journey to places our spirits can see,
Then, we will set our feet
in the places designed for them.
Lord, remind us there is your light in us
so, when our hearts need assuring
as we walk down the paths
that lead us through a valley of giants,
we'll have courage, vitality, and strength.
Lord empower us to trust the skills you've given us
and not to second guess ourselves
through uncertainty or fear.
Let the light shine in us joyfully
to make our souls sing songs during our darkest moments,
causing our hearts to celebrate, regardless of troubles.
Let the light in us be so empowering
that while in the middle of our worst encounter
the storm winds look at us confused
wondering at how we kept such resolve.

"So, I repeat," said the Wise Man with a warm, hearty smile
on his face and a glow in his demeanor.

"We all have a gift inside of us as powerful as light, and God placed it there. If you discover your gift, you'll be able to accomplish your assignment on earth and be empowered while you do it. However, there is also a crucial thing I want to mention. Although we all have a gift from God, and a particular purpose, no one can use their gift to its highest potential if they are not connected to Christ. In him, the gift gets its fullest value. Therefore, I pray everyone will discover their gift and use it for the glory of God, humanity, and themselves."

The Wise Man shifted on the edge of the chair again and said, "I know my gift and my purpose, but I have been challenged many times by those who don't believe that our unique gift comes from God. Also, I have been questioned by others who struggle with finding their purpose. So, I admit I can't convince everyone God made them unique and has given them a gift, but when I used to lose focus of the fact that I am unique with a special gift, I would look up and say …

Because of You

Because of you Lord there are mountain tops and waterfalls
and flatlands and valleys and rocks large and small
and rivers that flow and winds that blow
and seasons that change
and the snow that falls fast and slow, sunshine and rain.
There are undulating hills and daffodils
and dolphins and lions and whales
and graceful giraffes and baby calves
and elephants and monkeys and seals.
There are pebbles and sand and canyons grand
and the deserts hot and dusty.
There are stars in the sky and birds that fly
and moss on trees gray and musty.
There are snakes and snails and bobtails
and zebras and kangaroos,
and gorillas and koalas and gnats and flies
and colorful cockatoos.
There are angelic bodies and physical bodies
and then there's the human anatomy,
with ears to hear and eyes to see
and, the lungs that breathe and a mouth that inhales air,
There's the spinal cord, the circular system and
the left and right cerebral.
There are the feet and toes that man uses to go
walking through the terrestrial.
There are atoms and protons and molecules

and the force science calls inertia.
There are bones and blood cells, tissues and veins
and that which science calls plasma.
And all these things are because of you,
your hand has fashioned everyone,
and it only took you six days
and your work was completely done.
And it was good,
and nothing less than good, shall it ever be,
for your power is displayed on earth in grandeur
and in the whole of eternity.

The Wise Man took a sip of water and continued speaking. "I hope my actions will be useful for anyone here that may have lost focus of God, creating you for a specific reason. And, for those of you that don't believe that He created you with an individual purpose in mind, I hope you'll come to accept it as truth."

"I reminded myself of his grandeur every time I lost focus and would say to myself, 'All is well because of you God. All is well because of you!' That thought would settle and calm me in a way I can't explain, and it still does."

"So, you wholeheartedly believe that God made everything, every single thing?" a listener asked the Wise Man, curiously.

"I do," said the Wise Man cheerfully, as he stood up and began pointing at different things within the room.

"There is no escaping this fact. There is no need for a debate because we would all come to the same conclusion that all things come from an ultimate source. Look in any direction you choose. You're looking at the mind of God or man, and sometimes a combination of both. God created all things, and man-made everything from the resources made available to him."

"Yes, I believe that everything comes from an ultimate source," said the listener, "but I am not sure what that source is."

"That's where humanity gets stuck," said the Wise Man. "The disagreement arises because of the different opinions of what to call the source beyond man: the origin of ultimate creation."

"The argument is always about who or what should get the credit for the beginning of all things. But, no matter how anyone looks at it, the truth remains; we did not create ourselves. If we designed ourselves, we would have the power to keep ourselves from dying." "That's very true," said the listener pleasantly, "but it would sure be nice to discover the exact origin of man."

The Wise Man began pointing again, but this time he pointed at people in the room. "Excuse me for pointing at you, but when I look at creation," the Wise Man paused briefly to add emphasis to his words. "I find it too amazing to give credit to anything but an infinite creator."

"I call that fantastic creator Elohim; Jehovah-Elohim because that's what he says his name is. The intricate design of everything known to man is too amazing to not have an infinite creator. Therefore, I choose to remind myself that He would not take time to make things with such beauty and intricate detail and not have a specific purpose for it. It just wouldn't make sense." "I guess I can see that," said the listener reflectively.

The Wise man looked around slowly and said, "Let me add this for any others here who are not inclined to accept creationism as your belief. Even the Big Bang theorists and those inclined to embrace the 'evolutionary process,' would have to unanimously agree that people were placed on earth with a particular purpose."

As the Wise Man spoke, his face beamed gracefully and his smile emitted gratitude and portrayed his contentment. It was a smile of enjoyment as he reflected on the majesty and beauty that God had placed in the earth and that everyone had a specific purpose.

The Wise Man looked solemnly at the man who had asked him if he believed God made everything, and said, "I pray you will find conclusions in your search for truth."

"So, do I," he replied.

A small child ran forward to him and hugged his leg. She stretched out her arms for him to pick her up. He laughed and said, "What do you want, little lady?"

"Pick me up, Pawpaw, please! please, Pawpaw, pick me up!"

The Wise Man chuckled, picked up the child and said, "I love you," while rubbing his nose against her nose. She patted him on his forehead, which made his eyes crinkle and his head fall back. When he brought his head forward, their noses touched again. The Wise Man said playfully, "Someday you're gonna discover your purpose, little lady." She giggled and hugged him tightly.

The Wise Man shifted his gaze back to the listeners and spoke joyfully. "Life is a beautiful thing. Sometimes we forget to enjoy the small things presented to us because we focus most of our attention on what society considers essential. But, most of the things that we give significance to are material in nature and temporal. Our lives get overrun by the magic wand of possessions or the media's view of how we should live. The grind of making a living and the need to have more. All of these things become our motivators. Hypnotic idols! Have you ever noticed some of the most precious things you'll ever receive cannot be purchased by money?"

"My granddaughter's hug was priceless; I couldn't pay for it with all the gold in China. So, I've come to realize the joy and gratitude we express when experiencing something we consider essential should be the same as when we experience something seemingly menial. A mountain is just a stack of pebbles; minuscule is at the base of enormous. Therefore, we should be as excited over a pebble as we are about a mountain, as excited about a hug as we are about a paycheck, as overjoyed about a smile as we are about a new house."

The Wise Man smiled broadly and continued. "However, the general views of humanity are often off balance when it comes to appreciating things that seem insignificant. Our society is basically charmed by the grandiose, the spectacular, and the profound, not simplicity. We are often so busy and caught up with our quests for temporal achievements, momentary satisfaction, and the next big boom, that we often overlook the wonderful balance of the minuscule and majestic comingling all around us. And, the profundity God placed in it. There is an enormous benefit in having balance. Being able to appreciate the small and the grand, the temporary and the eternal, is a blessing we don't want to overlook."

"God is always trying to show us the incredible beauty in balance. For example, he lets the rain fall from heaven and it's absorbed in the earth. He makes the mist leave the grass and return to the heavens. Leaves fall off trees, and cover and protect the soil, as well as fertilize it. He gives lions, tigers, and other predators an excellent ability to be quiet and stealthy. But he gives the animals they hunt an amazing hearing ability or some other keen instinct and sense for danger. Think about the balance," said the Wise Man. "A circle of balance! Think about this: old folks have insight, an instinctive caution and usually go to bed early. Meanwhile, young people have vitality, a crazy curiosity and like staying up late. Balance is important in all areas of human existence so we can properly appreciate all things. Sadly, society often has its priorities upside down, so we lose balance and become stressed out and pressured."

"I believe that's why we are in such a hurry all the time. It seems we are trying to outrun time to accomplish as many temporal things as possible. Things become trivial when they do not have eternal worth; Eternal worth gives things lasting value. We need God to open our eyes to see it. There is the possibility of eternal worth in everything around us. My granddaughter's hug had eternal value because it was pure and full of love. Love is always eternal and, balance is an essential element of life!"

The Wise Man laughed thoughtfully. "We often take things for granted. No matter if the rain falls or the sun shines, the earth is refreshed. Life can be golden in the small and the big, in the positives and in what we sometimes see as negatives. We just need to open our hearts and take a closer look. Everything from the shapes of clouds to the trees blowing in the wind; it was all placed here for our enjoyment, but it's also here to show us balance. We have so many reasons to be thankful for what seems small and momentous in life."

"I suggest we slow down a notch or two and let everything find its natural flow; we could discover greatness in everything around us and be more content as we live out our purpose.

Without question, everything will change naturally by design, so why do we keep trying to speed up every process? Rush, rush, -rush! Hurry up, hurry up! Microwave it all!" He chuckled and continued. "Wouldn't it be better if we would learn to be patient; not procrastinate but be patient enough to let things take their natural course."

"Humans are in such a hurry! Where are we going on this earth that we must get there so fast?" The Wise Man laughed at his comment and a few others found it amusing also. "Seriously! Why are people in such a hurry? What will be will be, in time anyway, so why are we placing so much pressure on ourselves? Aren't we losing our leaves fast enough? Since we don't get to keep any of the things we accumulate on earth, wouldn't it make better sense to use our hammer, nails, baton, and ball in ways that show balance?"

"Job was speaking very pointedly when he said, 'Naked, I came into this world, and naked, I shall return to the grave.'

And according to wise Solomon, time and chance happen to everyone on earth. So, wouldn't it be much better to slow down and realize life is much more beautiful when we stop trying to force life's hand? When we view momentary experiences with the broader lens of eternity, things look very different," the Wise Man continued reflectively.

Providence, Fate, and Destiny!

Providence, mysterious providence,
where are you leading me now?
I can't see the end, but I'm pulled by your persuasion.
You're whispering to my soul, beckoning me to follow you
around another corner and over another obstacle.
In courage or uncertainty, I go step by step,
but I must admit my path has been riddled with much heartache
and although it hurts me to continue, quitting won't relieve
the pain so, I give myself a pep talk and hope for good again.
Fate, clever fate, where are you taking me now?
Because I feel you challenging me to look beyond the surface
of every up or down to focus on the center.
I also feel you encouraging me and filling me with contentment
as you move ahead, inviting me to trust you even more.
I'm getting a new desire to let you control my thinking
until I'm surrendered to your character and your course.
So, destiny, powerful destiny! If I promise not to question you,
will you promise to encourage me when you scratch or
shake my soul?

Two Sides of the Ground

Above the soil
are the tears and laughs and pain!
Joy and sorrow and success,
failure and progress and digression,
opportunities and riches and poverty,
famine and fullness and lack
and every earthly situation
that leaves a man still vertical
in the plain of the terrestrial.
Like toil and hustle and setbacks,
and pushing and shoving and giving,
and taking and lending and borrowing,
and hoping and waiting and quitting,
and holding and sharing and hating
that no one will do beneath the ground.
But continuing above the ground
will be plans being made,
and opportunities got and missed,
and good times being had,
and hard times being faced,
and memories being shared,
and appointments and makeups and breakups,
and friends and family and enemies,
and decisions and doubts and obstacles,
and adventures and hobbies and duties,
the continuance of life's familiarities.

And all the daily occurrences
which sometimes distract the person
from living in light of the most significant experience
that is possible because
Jesus overcame the power of the ground.

"Therefore, I repeat," said the Wise Man. "Slow down and reflect on your deepest desires because the primary overpowering mindset of most people is to continuously work on and for temporal things; things they cannot keep and much less take with them beyond the grave. Items that have no eternal value. It would be wise for all humanity to work towards things that last, things that are timeless, not temporal."

"This does not mean we are not supposed to enjoy life; we should enjoy life and every breath we have in it. However, we should be living life in a way that says we are aware of something greater. We don't have to live in a hurry trying to force things or manipulate things into place because some things are destined to happen. Ultimately there is nothing we can do to stop it or speed it up."

"The natural process of God," said Lodia interjecting her thoughts, "is beyond our control. It does its own thing without our help whether we like it or not. For everything, there is a season. Solomon tells us that in Ecclesiastes. It's incredible that in the very mouth that we use to eat and speak is the tongue. It develops new taste buds every seven years or so. So, a change will take place in us and all around us if we let it take its course. However, patience is a virtue not quickly developed or maintained. Especially in the climate today, society craves everything immediately. And if possible, they want it yesterday before yesterday arrives." Soft chuckles filled the room.

"That's my sentiments exactly!" replied the Wise Man. "God has determined a time for everything, and everything he destines shall come to pass. People can produce things by scientific manipulation, graphing, or using artificial intelligence, but it still takes time to go forward in the process of development and the eternal God still stands over time." So, as I suggested earlier, we should all give our lives to the Lord. We find our fullest potential in Him, and by following that course our abilities are used more positively, the goals we set will have a different motivation, and our lives affect other's lives in a more significant way. It's so powerful! It becomes the push in the soul and the fire deep in the heart. The determination is no longer just for an overnight sensation but a deep motivation to accomplish everything you are designed to do, as you enjoy your life with balance."

"When you know your real purpose and commit it to the Lord, strive daily to be productive for Him, the ball, the hammer, the nails, and the baton become transformative. It's like the moment that Mrs. Silverspoon spoke of when that solitary raindrop falls on your face, and the extraordinary happens. The remarkable illumination that you don't have to be in a rush. The fabulous revelation that being busy for the Lord is the best form of activity possible. The simple enlightenment that you may enjoy things that seem to be small and insignificant because they are placed in our lives by God. What a great reminder that there can be something great in something small. But the greatest revelation of all is this, compared to what's beyond this momentary existence, the earth can only offer little peanuts. That's the power in the raindrop moment and a surrendered life to the Lord."

"I give you this warning," the Wise Man said smiling. "When anyone moves forward in God's purpose or seeks to follow the destiny God has set for them, they will have to be careful of the traps and the pitfalls of getting sidetracked in the comfort zone. The comfort zone has many tricks. So, stay focused, humble, and determined, and then the road ahead of you will be a path of success. The dips, curves and bends will bring triumph, and although you will face some tragedies, some of those troubles will be the winds that push you the furthest."

The Wise Man paused, scratched his head, and continued. "Some of the most challenging experiences in my life have been the most beneficial. I had to fight myself just to get through but when you know your purpose and the one who gave it to you, it will push you forward even when you want to quit."

"I encourage everyone to not allow complacency to become your crutch because then you will forget to move steadily in the direction of better. We never have to be in a rush; we must only be consistent and faithful to the plan God has for our life. People following God's destiny must not get sidetracked by the masses that are plowing a road for themselves. Destiny always brings challenges, but we must be willing to keep moving in the right direction."

The Wise Man cleared his throat, took one last sip of water, and asked a question. "Is there anyone here that desires to get a fresh wind? You'd like to start something new beyond the fields that you have become accustomed to, knowing there is a broader horizon? Then move," he said, smiling broadly "and even if it isn't about starting something new but finishing something you've already begun, move forward with tenacity in that.

I encourage you, because often people are afraid to pursue new things in life. We are frightened to take that new challenge or follow that new adventure or walk that winding road with all the blind spots, and potholes in it."

"The river of life is before us, but how shall there be any progress if we keep shunning away from extraordinary challenges? What would life be like had abolitionists felt slavery was not a worthy cause to fight to end? What if Martin Luther King had been too scared to move in the direction of his dream, or had Rosa Parks given her seat up? What if Joan of Arc felt inadequate because she was a female? Or, if Mother Theresa would have viewed luxury more valuable than reaching out to those in poverty and need? What if Nelson Mandela would have cherished his freedom more than the freedom of a nation? Or, if Anne Frank would have given up in her horrible situation? And, what if Jesus would have quit on his way to the cross? Maybe these are things we should consider when faced with throwing in the towel or not making that move that's been pushing at our soul. The drive that's saying you can be the change that others need to see, is the same drive you should let take control of your actions."

"I know, sometimes it's hard to be a leader. It's tough to stay moving forward with a positive spirit and attitude when the odds are stacked against you. But, believe it or not, there's a game changer in everyone; it's in the DNA of humanity, and God put it there so we can be agents of change. For change only happens when you do."

"Therefore, I encourage and challenge you to consider and not forget, although we are following someone today, we may be leading someone tomorrow. Since our lives are intertwined and connected to each other's, let's reach out to someone of another race and culture and embrace them. Let's be that link that helps make the next link better. Let's make this the day that we think of someone other than ourselves. And by all means, let's get away from harming each other; we've done enough of that already! There is an image we all have in our mind of what we want the world to be like, and if we join in love, and never give up, it can head in that direction. My sincere hope and desires are to be more like Jesus with each breath I take. I'm striving to be a bridge of unity, not a wall of separation! Ask yourself what your deepest desire is and what you are doing to accomplish it."

The Wise Man shifted his stance and moved his eyes towards the steps that would take him down into the gatherers. He paused briefly, took one last deep breath, and refocused his attention on the audience. He wiped his eyes with a tissue and said very endearingly ...

"It would be impossible to thoroughly express the gratitude and appreciation I feel towards you at this moment, I sincerely thank you for coming. Your presence has been very encouraging.

And, as I look back in retrospect, the shotgun house was shaping me, the bells were teaching me, and the struggles were helping me in becoming who I am."

"Every valley that I went through, every mountain that I climbed, and every hole I fell into was an aide. It was beneficial and not nearly as hurtful as I look back reflectively as I thought it was in real-time. Time managed to bring healing, comfort, and a different perspective, but I had to learn to let go. Many people crave better while holding onto the negative and the lesser. However, to get the best, our minds, hands, and hearts must have the room open and available to facilitate increase."

"I learned that some of my hurts, troubles, and setbacks emptied me of the very thing that was blocking advancement." The Wise Man cleared his throat with a slight cough and continued. "Until tragedy struck, and the big problem came, I didn't know I could endure to that degree. I had not considered as sincerely the hurts and troubles of others, nor the pain they suffered until I experienced a great sorrow of my own. I hadn't looked at the tragedies and crises of the others in the adjoining room as carefully and as concerned as I do now."

"Now I am grateful for every moment, and I see life in breaths and as passing fields. I take myself down by the streams from time to time and remind myself there is always a new beginning, a chance to do better, and an opportunity to grow. I see that faith is necessary to go around, tear down, or climb over walls. I'm always acutely aware there are two sides of the ground."

"I know Golgotha was ugly; Calvary was necessary, and it was due to man desiring just one taste of the forbidden. So, I practice daily to ensure that the lyrics are good in my song. I often wrestle the inside man who attempts to distract and discourage me from living with hopes expectations and from keeping the faith given to me to succeed. Yes, it is obvious to me," continued the Wise Man, "that we are our own worst enemies, and no one can hold us back as much as we do ourselves. And, since we are often pros at procrastination and have the tendency to live in the land of hypocrisy, I pray for strength and guidance to stay away from these and the tag-team duo. I refuse to hang onto the dark days of America, although I am keenly aware, we still face racial problems today. Nevertheless, I will not falsely believe things cannot get better. I know a better day is always on the horizon, and a different way is always within reach."

The Wise Man wiped his eyes again and continued. "Remember to love and enjoy your time with friends and family, and with all the energy you can muster, make the best of every relationship. Because the road to true love and friendship is a rollercoaster ride that is worth every moment. Yes, there will be fools we encounter in this life, and there will be bridges we must cross as well as giants we will face. But, as we journey through our meadows and encounter every mountain, consider love always loves, which is essential in the God-blessed life." The Wise Man moved forward towards the steps at the end of the podium as his granddaughter trailed closely behind him, mimicking his moves and waving like a princess in a beauty pageant.

"While opportunities are available," he said sincerely, "do good and be kind to every man with all the energy in you and know you will receive a return on the investment you are making; for good is always rewarded. And, as you reflect on the fuel for thought, never forget you are well known by the God that sits in heaven, which is the ultimate power of one, ruling over the earth and all its splendor. If we practice never settling for less, nor trying to live in the comfort zone, we can face every day with a smile. Perspective always makes the difference so please live considering eternity. Because

Temporary

Life moves quickly as lightning flashing across the sky,
and is as intriguing and mysterious as the firefly.
It puts all mankind in the same river;
the rich and the poor are floating in the same direction.
And every day they're placing their affections
in that which they truly desire.
God placed us in time's hands
and with each passing moment, we lose feathers.
Feathers, once full of beauty and splendor
will become tattered and torn by the weather.
The grandeur of man on earth shoots by
as quickly as does light so it's sort of scary.
Yet, humanity is foolishly chasing the fleeting temporary.
Life is moving like an eagle in flight
and is as mysterious as a caterpillar becoming a butterfly.
It takes dips then rises to unimaginable heights.
It does things that confound us and presents truth undeniable.
We chase life as it hurries a few steps ahead of us
with every step we take, we lose earthly glory.
So, whether those steps are by wise men or fools,
every step is moving man towards another story.
A man's earthly grandeur expires so fast
it makes me hold my breath so it's sort of scary.
But, instead of humanity focusing on forever,
they have glued their eyes to a grand temporary.

The Wise Man paused, looked down at his granddaughter, gently took her hand, and walked down the steps of the podium. He took one last look around at those that had gathered, then continued speaking his final sentiments. "Thank you for your time and patience as you listened to my story and shared in my experiences. Thank you for your smiles, laughter, and tears. Thank you for your questions and comments, your challenges and your views which you shared with me in response to those I shared with you."

"I sincerely hope that something I said today will impact your lives and that it will challenge you to have a more open mindset, as you continue your life's journey. Perhaps I've said something positive enough and provoking enough for you to share it with others."

"I sincerely pray our encounter will produce seeds which bring forth an abundance of fruit. And that our lives will be like bees which pollinate flowers as they move throughout the field.

And, most importantly, may our lives be a reflection of a deep and meaningful relationship with the Father of all eternity through Jesus Christ. To sum up my philosophy in a capsule, I say that humanity needs Jesus more than anything else, you won't get anywhere if you don't move, one step in faith carries us further than any step in doubt; and our choices can produce junk or jewelry for ourselves and others. Therefore, always remember Life can be as enjoyable as paradise, however from the choices we make, it can be disastrous."

The room filled with a roar of applause as the Wise Man waved his hand in the gesture of thanks again. He picked up his grandchild and continued his journey with her as they headed toward the door.

REFERENCES:

Lao Tzu Quotes (n.d.). *The Journey of a thousand miles.* Brainy Quote. Retrieved from https://www.brainyQuote.com/quote/lao_tzu_137141

Baldwin, J. A. (n.d.). *These are all our children.* AZ Quotes. Retrieved from https://www.azquotes.com/quote/370515

Luther, M. (n.d.). *Just because a bird flies over your head.* Goodreads. Retrieved from https://www.goodreads.com/quotes/757798-you-cannot-keep-birds-from-flying-over-your-head-but

Ben-Menahem, A. (2006). *Baruch Spinoza. Sed Omnia.* Historical Encyclopedia of National and Mathematical Sciences. Retrieved from https://books.google.com/books?id=9tYrarQYhKMC&dq=Baruch+Spinoza,+Sed+Omnia&source=gbs_navlinks_s

Harvey, R. (2005). *Becoming Behavior.* Morris Publishing, Kearney, NE